TAMING A TEXAS BAD BOY

Copyright © 2019 by Katie Lane

Printed in the USA.

Cover Design and Interior Format

© THE KILLION GROUP INC.

# Taming a
# TEXAS
# BAD BOY

Bad Boy
Ranch
BOOK 1

# KATIE LANE

*To Christopher Carl, your jokes and
kind heart will be missed*

# CHAPTER ONE

EVERYTHING LOOKED EXACTLY AS CRU Cassidy remembered it. Flat, rocky buttes jutted up to the vibrant blue skies while shadowy, dark ravines carved their way down into the reddish-brown earth. Full junipers and straggly mesquite trees sprang from the rich soil. As did the native grasses that grew as high as wheat along the rusty barbwire fences. They waved in the stiff spring breeze like a big ol' Texas hello as Cru sped past. Not a soul traveled on the two-lane highway, and he took advantage of the fact by pressing down a little harder on the gas pedal. His Porsche 911 growled like a hungry cougar suddenly released from its cage, and he grinned as the tires ate up the narrow blacktop.

Cru was addicted to speed. The faster things went, the better. He loved fast cars, fast food, and fast women. Of course, sometimes fast could get you into trouble, a lesson Father Stephen at the St. James's Home for Children had tried, unsuccessfully, to teach him.

The thought of Father Stephen caused his joy to fade. He would miss the old priest. While he'd been too busy with the home to give Cru a lot of attention, he'd always been kind. And Cru knew he hadn't been an easy kid to be kind to. He glanced at the glove compartment. He didn't know why he'd brought the letter along. Especially when the person who wrote it meant nothing to him.

Absolutely nothing.

He pressed a little harder on the accelerator and cranked up the country satellite station he was listening to. He was so busy singing along with Blake Shelton about the love of a good woman that he missed the turnoff . . . almost. He took it going fifty, fishtailing and kicking up a billow of red dust and gravel.

He laughed and kept the pedal to the metal. But his laughter died when he sped out of the dust cloud and spotted a horse and rider crossing the dirt road. He slammed on the brakes and cranked the steering wheel, but not in time. The car skidded sideways straight toward the wild-eyed horse. Luckily, the black stallion jumped out of the way at the last second. Once the car came to a jarring halt, Cru hopped out of the car to apologize. Apologizing was his forte. He'd had to do it a lot in his life and he'd acquired a way with words. But when he got a good look at the rider, he was struck speechless.

The person struggling to calm the frightened horse was a beautiful woman. Not beautiful like the women Cru dated. Those women were almost too perfect. The better part of their days were spent following crazy diets, sculpting their bodies at a gym, enhancing their features at a makeup counter or with a plastic surgeon, and picking out just the right clothes. This woman's beauty was natural—like she had been formed from the world around her.

Her wild mass of hair was a mix of the deep burnt red of the clay soil and the glittering golden rays of the sun. Her eyes were the brilliant, unmarred blue of the Texas sky. And her lips the soft blush of the blooming spring flowers.

But her physical features didn't intrigue him as much as the way she handled the horse. The big black stallion continued to dance and rear, but she didn't seem concerned. She kept a tight hold on the reins and a secure seat in the saddle. When she spoke, her voice didn't hold a trace of fear. It was firm, yet soothing.

"It's okay, Severus. Calm down, baby. I'm right here."

Cru wasn't surprised the horse calmed. If he had been beneath her, he would take her instructions too. He never had a problem giving women control in bed. And if he played his cards right, he might just end up between the sheets with this fiery-haired cowgirl.

He pinned on his most charming smile. "Severus? Are we talking the evil Professor Snape from *Harry Potter*?"

She completely ignored him and continued to focus on the horse. "That's it." She stroked the horse's withers. "Just relax. You can't let some irresponsible jerk get you upset."

Irresponsible jerk? Cru's smile got even bigger. He liked feisty women. He took off his new Resistol straw cowboy hat and held it over his heart. "You're absolutely right, ma'am. I had no business taking that turn so fast. And I'm truly sorry for upsetting your villainous horse."

She dismounted in one graceful movement and picked up a battered cowboy hat that looked like it had seen better days. She dusted it off on her leg and strode toward him, her sky-blue eyes snapping with temper.

"If you'd read the entire series, you'd know that Severus wasn't a villain," she said. "He was a misunderstood hero who—" She cut off and those eyes widened with surprise. Cru smiled. After years of striking women speechless, he'd figured out that females liked his looks. Which worked out well for him because he liked females.

Since she couldn't seem to speak, he did. "I didn't read the series, but I did see the movies. While Snape was only doing what Dumbledore asked him to, he was still a real asshole to Harry. Not that Harry is my favorite character, mind you. The kid is a little too morose for me. I loved the Weasley twins. Now those two knew how to enjoy life."

As he talked, he took in every one of her features: the high forehead, the delicately arched eyebrows, the cute nose with its sprinkle of freckles, the stubborn chin, and the bowed mouth that was the prettiest pink he'd ever seen. Although the full lips looked a little chapped and he suddenly had the strong desire to give them moisture . . . with his mouth. Instead, he lifted a finger and brushed off the streak of dirt on her cheek. "You have a little—" Before he could finish, she jerked away and stepped back.

"Don't touch me, Cru Cassidy. Don't ever touch me again."

She tugged on her hat and swung back up on her horse before he could get over the shock that she knew his name.

"Wait! How do you know me?"

She wheeled the horse in the opposite direction. "You figure it out." She made a clicking sound and the animal responded better than Cru's Porsche. He had to jump out of the way as the horse took off.

He stood there watching that flame of fiery hair grow smaller and smaller and tried to figure out where he'd met the woman and how he had pissed her off. He usually didn't piss women off. They would get upset when he ended things. But he always talked his way out of any long-lasting hurt feelings—mostly because he never made promises he had no intentions of keeping. He was out for a good time and a good time only. And he always made that perfectly clear.

As he climbed back in his car and continued down the road, he puzzled over how he knew the redhead. He'd only spent one summer in this area when he was fifteen. And the only girl he could remember from that summer was a pretty blonde with a great set of tits. Ava. No, Evie. Evie Gardener.

Evie had been sexy as hell and he'd wanted to touch her phenomenal boobs in a bad way. He spent most of his summer working his charms on her. But he'd never tried to charm a feisty redhead. He would've remembered that.

He reached the fork in the road and took the left tine. After only half a mile, he saw the entrance to the ranch. He wasn't a sentimental type of guy. He'd learned long ago that getting attached to anything only caused unnecessary pain. But he couldn't help the twinge of something that felt a lot like sentimentally when he saw the rusty metal sign with the two bucking broncos on either side of the Double Diamond Ranch.

Fifteen years earlier, he had felt only anger when he'd seen the sign. He'd been pissed about having to stay on a boys' ranch in the middle of nowhere when he could've spent the summer in Dallas with all his friends. But Father Stephen had thought it would be good for Cru to get away from the orphanage for a few months. Or maybe the Father just needed a break from Cru.

Once Father Stephen had driven under the entrance to the ranch, Cru had apologized for stealing money out of the collection plate and smoking a joint in the confessional and streaking naked through the nuns' quarters. But to no avail. The father had driven right up to the sprawling ranch house and dropped him off with the two brothers who ran the place, with only a pat on the shoulder and a "God be with you" before he hopped back in the parish Oldsmobile and took off as if the hounds of hell were after him.

Back then, Cru probably had acted like a hound from hell. And he hadn't really changed that much.

But the ranch had.

As he pulled up to the sprawling house, he was saddened to see the place in such disrepair. The front porch sagged, shingles were missing from the roof, and the paint on the siding was peeling and blistered from the sun. The barn looked just as pathetic. And what happened to the corral? All that was left were a few fence posts and a field of weeds.

He turned off the engine and got out, feeling completely blindsided by the state of the ranch. The Double Diamond had once been a thriving business, with a barn filled with horses and pastures filled with cattle. Inviting troubled teenagers here for the summer hadn't been a moneymaking project as much as a charitable act for the two brothers. They'd had a rough childhood and were going down a troubled path when an old rodeo cowboy had taken them under his wing. They had wanted to do the same for other boys who were struggling to find their way. Cru had to admit he'd learned a lot the one summer he'd spent there and thought about the two old cowboys often. He liked picturing them riding and roping and swapping rodeo stories around an open fire. Now, even the old fire pit was gone.

A slamming screen door had him turning to the house. The older brother, Chester, stood on the porch holding a double barrel shotgun. While the rest of the ranch looked completely different, Chester had changed very little. His skin still looked like the leather of a beat-up football and he still sported a handlebar mustache that drooped down past his chin—although now it was as white as the hair on his head. He was a small man, but wiry and strong. This was proven as he lifted the shotgun with one hand and pointed it at Cru.

"You got bid-ness here?"

He didn't know why the gruffly spoken words made his chest tighten. He ignored the feeling and smiled. "I was wondering if you had room for a delinquent kid."

"We don't take in boys no more. We only did it one summer before Hank Gardener and the townsfolk put a stop to it. Assholes." He spit out a stream of chewing tobacco that landed inches from Cru's boots.

Cru had known he and the other boys were the first group to come to the Double Diamond. He hadn't known they were the last. But it made sense. While Chester and Lucas had kept them in line most the time, there had been a few incidences in town and with the owner of the neighboring ranch.

"We *were* a little ornery that summer," he said.

Chester squinted at him, then shifted the gun to his other hand and pulled out a pair of glasses from the front pocket of his wrinkled western shirt. Once he had them on, he still had to take a few steps closer before he recognized Cru.

"Well, I'll be a monkey's uncle. If it ain't Cru Cassidy." He leaned the shotgun against the house and carefully made his way down the porch steps. The way he moved made Cru realize that, although he looked the same, Chester had gotten older.

"How are you, boy?" Chester thumped him on the shoulder. "You're a little sturdier than the skinny kid I remember."

"I'm good. How are you?"

Chester stared at him, his eyes magnified by the thick lenses. "My eyes ain't what they used to be. The doc says I need cataract surgery, but I ain't going under the knife for any young know-it-all doc." That was so like Chester. He had always been the stubborn one. The one who didn't listen to anybody and lived by his own set of rules.

Cru grinned. "I don't think they use a knife. I think it's a little more high-tech than that."

"High-tech. Hhmmph. That's even worse. I'm not having some space-age beam of destruction pointed at my eyes." Chester studied him. "So what are you doing in these parts? Last I heard you were selling cars in Dallas."

"I did sell cars for a while in Dallas. And in Houston, Austin, San Antonio, and Galveston. I'm what you call a traveling car salesman."

Chester snorted. "You always were an antsy kid."

It was the truth. Cru never could sit still. The nuns at the orphanage had been convinced he had an attention deficit disorder. And he probably did. But the way he'd felt the last two months was more than just antsy. Even when he was traveling, negotiating a deal on a car, or having wild sex with a beautiful woman, he felt like something just wasn't right. He probably could've ignored the feeling—he was good at ignoring feelings—if the chest pains hadn't started.

Worried he had a heart condition; he'd gone to see a doctor. But he'd passed all the tests with flying colors. So he'd decided it was Texas that was making him feel restless. He'd lived here for far too long. He needed to see more of the country. More of the world. He'd planned to start with California where the sand was as hot as the women. But then he'd spotted a road sign for Simple, Texas. The next thing he knew he was heading toward the Double Diamond Ranch.

"Well, I'm glad you stopped by to see a couple of old cowboys," Chester said. "Grab your gear and come on inside. I'll make you a cup of coffee."

Chester made the worst coffee this side of the Pecos and tried to pawn it off on everyone. When he was fifteen, Cru had drunk it without complaint to prove he was tough enough to handle strong black coffee that would curl your toes. Now he was willing to give up his pride and save the lining of his stomach.

"I'll pass on the coffee," he said. "I can't stay long. I'm on my way to California . . . to see a sick friend."

The disappointment on Chester's face was easy to read, and Cru started to wonder if stopping by had been a good idea. He didn't need to add guilt to his restlessness. Thankfully, Chester made light of it.

"No problem. All the spare rooms are filled with junk that Lucas has collected over the years anyway. I've never met such a hoarder in all my born days." He headed to the house and Cru hurried to help him up the steps, but he should've known better. Chester immediately swatted his hand away. "I'm not some feeble old man who needs help up a few stairs." But even as he said the words, he missed the first step and would've fallen if Cru hadn't steadied him.

Chester jerked off his glasses and crammed them in his shirt pocket. "Damn things. Can't see with them and can't see without them."

While the outside of the house looked different, the inside of the house looked much the same. The front entryway still held a bunch of hooks for coats and cowboy hats and a place beneath to store your boots. Since it was late March, Cru wasn't wearing a coat, but he put his hat on a hook, and then toed off his cowboy boots.

If on cue, Lucas's voice rang out from the kitchen. "You better not be tracking horse shit on my floors, Chester! Now hurry up. Lunch is almost ready."

Chester cringed. "Lord help us."

Cru was confused by Chester's remark. Lucas had always been an amazing cook. Cru had never eaten so well as when he'd stayed at the ranch. Lucas's meals were the kind that stuck to your ribs: buckwheat flapjacks piled high with real maple syrup and sausage or bacon on the side, thick porterhouse steaks straight off the cow with steaming baked potatoes and a side of brown sugar baked beans, and heaping bowls of Lucas's famous beef chili with thick slabs of cornbread covered in melting honey butter. Cru's mouth watered just thinking about all the meals he'd had there.

But when he walked into the kitchen, the smell that hit him didn't make his mouth water. It made him a little nauseous. Whatever was cooking smelled like burnt rubber. He glanced around and became even more confused. Lucas had always kept his kitchen immaculate, but now it looked like a class of kindergarteners had been cooking in it. There were pots and pans piled high in the sink, an inch of grease and spatter on the stove, and boxes and bottles of cooking ingredients cluttered the counter.

And Lucas looked even worse.

When Cru had spent the summer there, Lucas had always been clean-shaven, without a hair on his head out of place. His western shirts and Wranglers had been pressed to perfection and his boots polished to a mirrored gleam. Now, he looked like he'd just crawled out of bed. His hair was messed, his jaw unshaven, and his shirt wrinkled. But what concerned Cru the most was the way he limped over to the refrigerator.

When he spotted Cru, he froze. A big smile split his face. "Cru Cassidy." He limped over and pulled Cru into a tight hug. "Ain't you a sight for sore—"

The front screen door slammed, cutting him off and the fiery redhead strode into the kitchen. She didn't look surprised to see Cru there. Just annoyed.

But the annoyance drained from her pretty blue eyes when she turned them to Lucas and Chester. Her face softened with a smile that changed her from beautiful to breathtaking. There was something familiar about the smile. He did know her. Or, at least, her smile.

"How are my two favorite cowboys today?" She walked over and kissed Chester on the cheek before doing the same to Lucas and handing him a pharmacy bag. "Here's the muscle ointment you asked for. But I still think you should see a doctor." She glanced down at his ankle. "And until you do, you shouldn't be walking on it."

Lucas took the bag. "It's just a little ol' sprain. Don't you worry about this old man. Especially now that one of our boys is back." He glanced at Cru. "You remember Penny Gardener, don't you, Cru?"

It took a moment for the name to register. When it did, his eyes widened with surprise. He remembered the skinny little girl with braces who had trailed around after him all summer with adoring eyes. He just hadn't thought she'd grow into a sexy cowgirl who looked at him like he'd just crawled from beneath a rock.

"You're Evie's little sister?" he said. "The one who had the crush on me?"

It was the wrong thing to say. Those blue eyes flashed with temper. "That was before I knew what a jackass you were." She turned on a boot heel and walked out.

As soon as the screen door slammed behind

her, Chester and Lucas looked at each other and laughed before Chester lifted a white bushy eyebrow at Cru. "I'd say the crush is over."

# CHAPTER TWO

PENNY TUGGED HER COWBOY HAT low and urged Severus to a faster pace. But no matter how fast the stallion galloped, she couldn't outdistance all the rioting emotions that consumed her.

Cru Cassidy was back.

After fifteen years, he just showed up out of the blue in a sporty red car he drove like a maniac. Why was he here? What did he want? And how had he known she'd had a crush on him? Not even her sister knew that.

Her cheeks heated with embarrassment. Not just because Cru knew she'd had a crush on him, but also because she'd run off like the immature kid she'd once been. A mature woman would've acted like a childhood crush was no big deal and stayed to find out what he was doing there. But Penny hadn't felt like a mature woman. All it had taken was one look in Cru's eyes and she'd been catapulted back to the summer of her thirteenth year.

She'd been an awkward new teenager with

freckles, acne, and braces. Cru Cassidy had been fifteen and teen-idol gorgeous with hair as dark as a raven's wing, eyes as green as a rain-drenched meadow, and a smile as bright as the Texas sun.

But it wasn't his looks that started Penny's crush. It was the hot summer day she'd taken a jump she had no business taking and had fallen off her horse. The skittish mare had taken off, leaving Penny to hobble back to the ranch with a sprained ankle and a bruised ego. Cru had ridden up like a hero in an old western. She'd wanted to die from embarrassment. But instead of teasing her about being thrown, he'd helped her up on his horse and then remounted behind her. It was the first time she'd ever been in a boy's arms and she was stunned speechless. But Cru must've thought her silence and flushed cheeks had to do with her humiliation because, the entire way back to the Gardener Ranch, he regaled her with funny stories about his most embarrassing moments.

That was all it had taken for a naive thirteen-year-old to fall head over boots in love. But she never stood a chance with Cru Cassidy. He had set his sights on a prettier, smarter, and more mature girl.

Reining in Severus, Penny pulled her cellphone out of her front shirt pocket. Evie answered almost immediately.

"Hey, Pen. I was going to call you this morning, but things have been hectic here at the bank and I have to meet with the principal of Clint's high school this afternoon."

Penny knew why her sister had to meet with her nephew's high school principal. Clint had called her last night and given her the entire story. But she couldn't tell Evie that. Clint trusted her with things he felt like he couldn't share with his mother. And unless he was doing something harmful to himself or other people, Penny wouldn't break that trust.

"What happened?" she asked.

Evie released an exasperated sigh. "He was caught smoking on campus and got suspended. He claims he was only holding the cigarette for a friend while the kid bent down to tie his shoes, but he won't tell the principal who the friend is. According to Clint, the kid ran off when the campus cop showed up."

That was the same story Clint had told her. "And you don't believe him?"

"I want to, but he hasn't exactly been honest with me lately. He said he got a C on his geometry test and come to find out he got an F. He said he wouldn't hang out with that no-good Tommy Baker and I caught him talking to him the other night on the phone."

"Maybe Tommy called him. As for the geometry test, I think I remember both of us lying about our grades to Daddy."

"That was different. Daddy was a tyrant about us getting good grades. If we got anything less than an A, we were stuck cleaning out the horse stalls. And you know how much I hate cleaning up poop." While Penny loved being in the barn around horses, Evie was more of a homemaker. She loved to decorate, garden, and cook. Even with a fulltime job, she had turned her little house in Abilene, Texas, into a magazine-worthy home for her and Clint.

"Of course, he was never as tough on you," Evie continued.

"Only because I don't ever come straight at him. If you come straight at a bull, you're more than likely going to get gored in the belly. I prefer to circle around from behind and surprise him."

Evie laughed. "You always have been good with stubborn animals. And there's no doubt Daddy is as stubborn as they come."

"And you're just as stubborn. Which is why you two are constantly locking horns." And why Evie and Clint no longer lived on the ranch. Something Penny was trying hard to fix. "If both of you would just give a little, I'm sure you could stop this feud you're having."

"We're not having a feud. I just refuse to live on the Gardener Ranch under Hank Gardener's thumb, that's all."

"Are you saying I'm living under Daddy's thumb?" The pause was too long. "Evie! I'm not living under Daddy's thumb. I do what I want, when I want."

"No, you don't. You do what Daddy wants when he wants, but it seems to work for you. It doesn't work for me. I guess I am more like Daddy and you're more like Mama—willing to overlook his controlling nature."

"I can't always overlook it, but he's our father, Evie. And he loves you and wants you to come home. I love you and want you to come home too—if not to the ranch, at least to Simple where I can see you every day."

"I miss you too, Pen. But it's not just Daddy keeping me away. I have a job here, and friends . . . and Edward." She paused. "He asked me to marry him again."

"And I hope you said no. You told me yourself that you don't love him."

"But I like and respect him. At thirty, I've come to realize that those two emotions are more important than love. And maybe Clint would behave better if he had a firm stepdad who wasn't as much of a pushover as his mother."

"Clint doesn't need a firm hand," she said. "He's just a teenager sowing a few wild oats."

Evie laughed. "You sound like Lucas. He never thought any of the boys who showed up that one summer were troublemakers. They were all just sweet kids who had been dealt a bad hand. How is he?"

"Not good. He's still limping. Which makes me wonder if it's more than just a sprain. Not to mention his memory loss. He can no longer remember the recipes of dishes he's made forever. Poor Chester has been getting some pretty awful concoctions for meals."

"Do you think he's getting dementia?"

"I don't know. And there's no way to find out. Those two refuse to go to a doctor. I wish I had more time to check on them, but we lost a couple ranch hands and I have my hands full."

"Maybe they should hire someone. Or contact a relative who could help."

"You know they don't have any relatives or children of their own. Although the way they talk, you'd think the teenagers who came that summer where their kids." She paused. "And one did come back. Cru Cassidy." She waited for Evie's reaction. Any reaction. But her sister had always been good at keeping her emotions bottled up—unlike Penny, who wore her heart on her sleeve.

"Well, that's good. Maybe he can give Chester and Lucas the help they need. But you stay away from him, Pen. Those boys were all bad business."

"I have no plans of hanging out with Cru Cassidy. And I don't think he's here to help out. I would bet he just stopped by to show off his flashy Porsche." She wanted the words back as soon as she'd said them. Evie didn't need to know that Cru was flaunting his expensive car when her sister had spent so many years struggling to make ends meet. But Evie didn't seem to mind.

"Cru always talked about getting a fast car." She paused. "And if you do run into him, make sure you don't let anything slip, Pen. Now I need to go. I have a loan officers' meeting here at the bank before my meeting with the principal."

"Good luck with the principal. And for the record, I think you should believe Clint. He hasn't smoked since he got into Daddy's cigars when he was eight."

Evie groaned. "I've never had to clean up so much puke in my life."

Penny laughed. "I think it was a lesson well learned."

"You're probably right. I'll let you know how it goes with the principal. And whatever you do, don't tell Daddy. You know how he loves to stick his nose in my business, and I just can't deal with his controlling nature right now."

"Of course I won't tell him. See, we don't tell our parent everything either."

"Point taken. Love you, Pen."

"Love you too."

After ending the call, Penny felt much better. She had thought the news of Cru coming back for a visit might upset her sister. But it looked like Evie had moved on. She was right. What happened that summer was in the past. And everyone knew the past was best left there. Any feelings Penny had when she saw Cru were just remnants from her childhood. Nothing else.

Still, she planned to stay away from the Double Diamond Ranch until Cru left. While she would miss seeing Lucas and Chester, she had enough to deal with on her own ranch. Spring branding would start soon and it was always a busy time, especially when they were short on ranch hands. Of course, all seasons were busy, and Penny loved every single one of them.

The ranch was more than just a home. It was her life. Every day, she would wake up when the sun hadn't yet peeked over the horizon and say a prayer of thanks for getting to do what she loved. She loved spending her days outside with animals and nature. She loved riding or driving through miles and miles of beautiful country without seeing a billboard, or a building, or even a single soul.

What she didn't love was not having Evie and Clint there to enjoy the ranch with her. Evie might act like she loved living in the city, but Penny knew better. Evie rarely called without asking about the ranch or the townsfolk of Simple. It was obvious she missed her home, and Penny was willing to do whatever it took to get her sister back where she belonged. Even if she had to go up against their stubborn father.

And he was stubborn. Penny had no more than swung down from the saddle when he came storming out of the house. "Where have you been?"

Even at close to sixty, Hank Gardener was an intimidating man. He was well over six foot tall with broad shoulders and a fit body from working a ranch all his life. When he opened his mouth, he sounded even more intimidating. But Penny was used to his loud bluster.

"Checking the fences in the east pasture." She didn't mention stopping by the Double Diamond Ranch to drop off the ointment she'd gotten Lucas. Her father didn't get along with the Diamond brothers and would blow a gasket if he knew how much time she spent with the two old cowboys.

"Well, I'm glad you're back because you need to tell me what the hell this is?" He waved a sheet of paper at her.

"If you stop waving it around like a madman, I'll be happy to."

He sent her a stern look before he shoved the paper at her. She took one look and knew exactly what it was. "It's the invoice for our new website redesign. I told you about it."

"You told me that you wanted to tweak our website. You did not tell me that it was going to cost me two thousand dollars."

She tried to act surprised. "Are you sure? I could've sworn that I ran the number by you."

"You did not. If you had told me a few tweaks were going to cost me that much money, I would've said hell no. You acted like it was only going to cost a couple hundred."

"It was a little more than I expected."

"A little? A hundred is a little. Fifteen hundred is highway robbery. Especially to pay some computer geek for a dancing cow."

She bit back a smile. "So you took a look at the new website?"

"Of course I took a look at it. I wanted to see what cost me a small fortune. And I didn't see anything on there worth that kind of money."

Raul, one of the ranch hands, showed up and took Severus's reins, sending her a sympathetic look. "Let me take Severus back to the stables, Miss Penny."

"Thank you, Raul," she said. "How's your daughter's spring cold?"

"She still has a little fever, but my wife says she's feeling much better today."

"That's good to hear. I'll have Sadie send over some of her oatmeal cookies. I know Loretta loves them."

"Thank you, Miss Penny."

She waited until he was gone before she continued the argument with her father. "This isn't the old days, Dad, when you could put an ad in a rancher's magazine for a couple hundred dollars or get business cards printed up to hand out at a rancher's convention. Now, websites are the new business card. And they're a thousand times more effective because people all over the world can get on and see what we do here at the ranch. With just a few clicks, potential buyers can see our entire operation. And just like you didn't want to hand out cheap business cards or put up a cheap ad, you don't want our website to look cheap either. Putting together a good website takes expertise, hard work, and time. I promise it will be worth every penny. If it's not, you can take it out of my pay."

He studied her for a long moment. "You bet I will." He jerked the invoice out of her hand. "Now let's get inside and eat lunch so we can start going over the applicants for the new ranch hands and Sadie will stop badgering me about eating healthy. I swear I should've fired that woman a long time ago."

Penny climbed the steps of the porch. "Don't give me that. You wouldn't know what to do without Sadie."

"The hell I wouldn't. I'd live in peace and eat what I wanted to. That's what I'd do. My cholesterol is fine."

"No, it's not. The doctor says it's way too high.

And if Sadie left, what would you eat? Because neither one of us can cook."

He followed her into the house. "I survived before I married your mother on my cooking. I figure I can survive again."

As she hung up her hat in the hallway, she glanced at the picture of her mother that hung just above the line of hooks. Helen Marie Gardener had been just the opposite of her husband. She never raised her voice, never had an enemy, and never stopped smiling.

When she died, it was like all the sunshine had left the house. Penny had felt the loss of her mother deeply, and so had her father. They had both gone into a deep depression after Helen Marie had passed away. Hank had turned angry and brooding, while Penny had turned to her sister. It was Evie's love that pulled her out of her depression. Evie stepped into their mother's role, packing Penny's lunches for school, making sure she wore her hat in the winter, and helping her with her homework. At night, when Daddy was in bed and the house was quiet, Evie would sneak into Penny's bed and take out a picture of their mother. The same picture that now hung on the wall. They would hide under the covers and Evie would shine a flashlight on the picture and they'd talk for hours about all the special things they remembered about her.

As time when on, their grief lessened and they no longer had to talk about their mother to feel her love. Daddy hired Sadie to cook, clean, and watch out for them. But Evie still snuck into

Penny's room each night just to talk. They shared everything they couldn't share with their angry, grieving father. The only thing Evie had refused to share was the name of the boy who got her pregnant when she was fifteen.

But Penny knew. She had always known.

Cru Cassidy was the only boy who had blatantly chased after Evie that summer. The only boy who could easily make a girl forget her morals and take a walk on the wild side. And maybe that's why Penny had never told her sister she knew her secret. She didn't want Evie finding out she wasn't the only Gardener sister who had fallen for a Double Diamond bad boy.

The very same bad boy.

# CHAPTER THREE

THE SOUP LUCAS MADE FOR lunch was inedible. Cru was only able to choke down a few spoonfuls before he made the excuse of having eaten before he got there. Chester didn't make an excuse. After one bite, he declared it was the worst soup he'd ever eaten, which resulted in a huge argument between the brothers. Cru finally interceded with the only thing he knew would stop their fussing: He asked to see their rodeo trophies.

The soup feud was forgotten. For the next few hours, Cru sat on the dilapidated couch in the living room and listened while Chester and Lucas pointed out their rodeo belt buckles and trophies on the shelves above the television and told one story after the other. Cru had heard all their rodeo exploits the summer he was there, but he enjoyed hearing them again. Halfway through the story about how he'd busted his collarbone being tossed off a brahma bull named Tornado, Chester nodded off in his recliner. Lucas grumbled about him being an old fart who couldn't keep his eyes open, but a few minutes later, he joined his brother in a late afternoon nap.

It was the perfect opportunity to leave. But Cru couldn't leave without saying goodbye. Nor could he bring himself to wake them. So he quietly got to his feet and headed to the bathroom. The faucet in the bathtub dripped and it took three tries to get the toilet to flush. Obviously, the inside of the house needed as many repairs as the outside. Once he left the bathroom, he headed down the hallway and found the room he'd stayed in when he'd been there. Chester was right. The bedroom was filled with a bunch of junk, but the twin beds looked the same—right down to their blue chenille bedspreads and Cru's initials carved into the wooden headboard of one.

He moved the boxes of old books and record albums from the bed to the floor and lay down. He chuckled out loud when he saw the naked Playboy centerfold still taped to the ceiling. He'd been so smug when he'd pulled the magazine from his suitcase and showed it to the boy he was rooming with.

Logan McCord hadn't been impressed. He hadn't even asked to look at the magazine. Of course, he'd been a brooding James Dean type who hadn't been impressed by much. But regardless of his moody personality, he and Cru had hit it off and become the best of buddies that summer. Logan didn't say much, which worked out well for Cru, who loved to talk. They had remained friends over the years, calling each other to check in every few months.

And if there was ever a time to check in with a fellow Double Diamond boy, it was now.

Cru pulled out his cellphone. Logan answered in his usual blunt fashion.

"So you're still alive. I thought one of your many women might've strangled you in your sleep by now."

He laughed. "That's why I never spend the night with women." He glanced around. "So you'll never guess where I am."

"Jail."

Again he laughed. "You were the criminal who loved hot wiring old cars and taking them for joyrides. I was the law-abiding bad boy."

Logan snorted. "A real saint who shoplifted condoms."

"Only because I didn't want word getting back to Chester and Lucas that I was buying them. But they found out anyway when Mr. Sanders caught me stealing them from his store. Man, he was pissed. The entire town had been convinced we were nothing but a bunch of delinquents. Remember the nickname they gave the Double Diamond?"

"Bad Boy Ranch. And we were pretty bad the first few weeks we got there. I don't know how Chester and Lucas put up with us."

"Not just put up with us, but stuck up for us. Sanders would've turned me in to the sheriff if Chester hadn't shown up and talked him out of it. Of course, I still got a stern lecture on the drive back to the ranch about stealing. But a few weeks later, I found those condoms in my top drawer."

He smiled at the memory, but it was a bittersweet smile. "They aren't doing good, Logan."

"What do you mean?"

"I'm here at the Double Diamond. I was on my way to California and got a wild hair to see the two old cowboys. I thought they'd been ranching and enjoying life. But they aren't. They've sold all the cattle. Chester can barely see and Lucas has sprained his ankle and is limping around—not to mention that he's having trouble remembering things. Remember what a great cook he was? Well, now he makes beef vegetable soup with no beef and no vegetables. It was burnt broth with egg noodles." Just talking about food made Cru's stomach grumble with hunger and he rolled to his feet and headed to the kitchen to see if he could find something to eat besides leftover soup.

Logan blew out a breath. "Damn. Have they gone to see a doctor?"

Cru snuck past the living room where the two old cowboys were still napping. "The last doctor Chester saw told him he needed to get his cataracts removed, but Chester says there's nothing wrong with his eyes. Just like Lucas thinks his ankle only needs some time to heal. Which is probably true if he'd stay off it."

Cru went into the pantry to look for a jar of peanut butter to make a sandwich, but he only found a stick of deodorant, a pair of underwear, and canned goods. He spotted a can of kidney beans and it made him hungry for Lucas's chili. Lucas had taught him how to make chili and numerous other dishes. He hadn't wanted to learn how to cook, but being on kitchen duty was better than being on bathroom cleaning or stall mucking duty. And learning to cook had ultimately worked in his favor. It turned out that women couldn't resist a man who knew his way around a kitchen. He grabbed the can of beans and a can of tomato sauce before he left the pantry.

"Those two have always been stubborn," Logan said. "So they don't have any ranch hands to help them?"

"No, and the ranch shows it. It's falling down around their ears." He looked in the freezer for any kind of ground meat that he could use for chili. He found a package of ground beef, but he also found an Almanac and a pair of socks. It looked like Lucas wasn't just forgetting ingredients.

"I guess I just thought they'd be roping and riding forever," Logan said with sadness in his voice.

"Yeah, I know. But according to Chester, they only have one old mare who's too old to ride." Cru pulled Lucas's old cast iron Dutch oven out of the drawer beneath the stove. Lucas had cooked everything from bison pot roast to his famous chili in the seasoned pan. Now he probably didn't even remember where he'd put it. Cru placed the pan on the stove and turned the dial to light the burner. When it wouldn't light, he remembered that he needed to light it with a match. While he searched the drawers, Logan continued.

"Do you think they had to sell all the livestock because they're struggling financially?"

"It makes sense. If they're too old to ranch, all they have to live on is two social security checks." He found a lighter and lit the stove.

"I should've checked on them. They believed in me when no one else did."

Cru unwrapped the ground beef and put it in the pan. "Me too. They taught me more in three months than I'd learned the fifteen years before. So what do you think we should do to help them?"

"I don't know. But it sounds like they can't be left alone. Can you stay there and keep an eye on them until we can come up with a plan? I know it's a lot to ask. But I'm not asking you to do it indefinitely. Just until we can figure something out."

"Me? Why don't you come?"

"Because I opened a new auto repair shop and don't have the time. It sounds like you do."

"Well, I don't. I'm on my way to California."

"For work?"

He really wanted to lie. Instead, he stated the obvious. "Look, I'm not the man for this job. I'm the irresponsible one, remember? What about Holden? He was always the reliable one. And I bet he doesn't have a job to worry about. His family has more money than they know what to do with."

"Last I heard, he's estranged from his family and works fulltime representing people who can't afford an attorney."

"It figures. He was always a do-gooder. What about Lincoln, Val, or Sawyer?"

"You know that Val is busy writing his next bestselling thriller. And I don't have a clue how to get in touch with Linc or Sawyer." Logan paused. "Accept it, Cru. You're it."

Cru rubbed a hand over his face. Shit. This is what he got for being impulsive and taking the turn to Simple. "Fine. I'll stay for now. But we need to figure something out soon."

"We will. I'll do some research and see if I can't contact one of the other guys and get someone there to help you."

"Good. It will probably take more than me to convince Chester and Lucas that they can't continue to live here by themselves. They need to sell the ranch and move to one of those retirement communities on a golf course."

"You know they don't golf. And I can't see either one of those old cowboys leaving that ranch unless it's feet first. Is there someone in town we could pay to help them?"

"I'll look into it. Maybe Penny Gardener would be willing to do it. She seems to be fond of them. You remember Penny, don't you? She's Evie's younger sister." When Logan didn't say anything for a long time, Cru thought the call had dropped. "Logan? You there?"

"I remember."

Cru flipped the frozen meat so it could brown on the other side. "Evie was hard to forget. Although now that I think about it, I spent more time with Penny than with Evie. She followed me around everywhere telling me those stupid knock-knock jokes."

"If I remember correctly, you didn't seem to

mind. Her adoration stroked that gigantic ego of yours."

He had liked Penny's attention. She'd been a pretty cute kid. And now she was a stunning woman. "You can never have too much female attention. And I wouldn't mind Penny Gardener stroking something now. The little freckle-faced girl has grown into a beautiful woman—a little angry, but beautiful."

"You saw Penny? Was Evie there?"

"She might be at the ranch, but she wasn't there when I almost mowed Penny and her horse down with my Porsche."

"You're still reckless, I take it."

"I'm not reckless. As Lucas used to say, I'm just foot loose and fancy free."

"And a busy butt." Lucas's voice had Cru glancing over his shoulder to see the old guy scowling at him. He had always been possessive about his kitchen, and it looked like things hadn't changed. "What are you doing in my kitchen?" he snapped.

"I'll call you later," Cru told Logan before he hung up and turned to Lucas. "I had a craving for your famous Texas chili."

The scowl disappeared. "Well, why didn't you say so? I can have a pot whipped up in no time." Lucas's eyes squinted. "Now let's see. What do I need? Beans!" He headed to the pantry and returned with two cans of green beans.

Cru's stomach flip-flopped at just the thought of green bean chili. "Why don't you let me make the chili, Lucas? I haven't made it in a long time and I want to see if I remember the recipe. Besides, you shouldn't be standing on your sprained ankle. You don't want Penny getting mad at you, do you?"

Lucas hesitated for a moment before he nodded. "You're right. That little gal is as sweet as peach pie most the time, but she does has a wee bit of a temper." He handed the green beans to Cru and winked. "And today all that temper seemed to be directed at you."

Penny *had* been all fired up. And if Cru had learned anything about women over the years it was that they didn't usually get all fired up over men they didn't care about. Penny still felt something for Cru. And since he was stuck here, he might as well find out exactly what that was. He smiled. Suddenly, staying there for a while didn't seem like such a bad punishment.

He turned back to the stove and continued stirring the hamburger. "So how often does Penny stop by?"

"I can't remember what days people come callin'. She comes by a lot and more when me and Chester caught the flu last winter."

Cru glanced over his shoulder. "Don't you get the flu shot?"

"I'm not gettin' a needle stuck in my hide to keep me from getting a few sniffles." Lucas hobbled over to a chair and sat down.

"The flu shot isn't for colds, Lucas. It's for the kind of flu that kills people." He left the hamburger cooking and pulled out another chair. "Put your foot up." Once Lucas had his foot propped on the chair, Cru went to the freezer and took out a bag of frozen peas.

"Make sure to put those in the chili last or they get too mushy," Lucas said.

Cru rolled his eyes. "They aren't for the chili. They're for your foot." He placed the bag on Lucas's ankle before he went back to the stove. "Why haven't you hired a ranch hand to help around here?"

"You know how suspicious Chester is. He doesn't trust just anyone. And do you know what ranch hands charge now? Why, it's highway robbery."

So they *were* struggling to make ends meet.

"Maybe you could sell a few pieces of land," he said as he opened the can of beans with a hand held can opener. "Just enough to hire a ranch hand . . . and maybe a cook."

"I don't need anyone helping me cook. And I'm sure not going to sell my ranch to some yahoo like Hank Gardener."

He turned to Lucas. "Penny's dad offered to buy the ranch?"

"The jackass showed up here a month ago and made us an offer. As if we'd sell cow crap to that arrogant man. He's the reason we had to close down the boys' ranch after only one year. Hank got the town all riled up about us bringing in a bunch of delinquents to rape their daughters and pillage their stores."

Hank Gardener might be an arrogant jerk, but selling the ranch to him would solve all of Chester and Lucas's problems. With the money, they could buy a place anywhere they wanted to. Maybe they could even keep the land the house was on and hire someone to help them. Now all Cru had to do was convince them.

"But Penny is Hank's daughter," he said. "I thought you liked her."

Lucas snorted. "If I thought Penny or her sister Evie had a say in running the Gardener Ranch, I might think about selling Hank the north pasture he's so interested in. But the man doesn't let those girls have a say in anything. He ran Evie off with his mule headedness and treats poor Penny like an employee instead of a daughter."

"Where did Evie move?"

"She lives in Abilene with her son. And as much as I love Penny, I wish she'd join her. A flower can't grow in the shade of an old oak. She needs to get out from her father's shadow and become her own woman."

Cru started adding spices to the chili. "She looked like she was her own woman to me." A feisty woman who would probably be just as feisty in bed.

"On the outside maybe, but on the inside, she's still an insecure little girl hoping to gain her father's love after she lost her mother. It's hard to go without a mama and daddy's love. Their love is what shapes you growing up."

Which probably explained why Cru was so misshapen. He'd gone without both.

Chester shuffled into the kitchen and sniffed the air. "What's cookin'? It actually smells good for a change."

Lucas immediately bristled. "How would you know if somethin' smells good, you old fart? Your sense of smell is as bad as your eyesight."

"Well, my sense of taste is just fine. And there was no beef or vegetables in that beef vegetable soup, you ornery old cuss. Just limp noodles."

Before things could escalate, Cru jumped in. "It's probably good we didn't eat beef for lunch because I put plenty in the chili we're having for supper."

Chester turned to him with surprised. "You stayin' for supper, boy? What happened to your sick friend in California?"

"He just called and said he's doing better. So if it's okay with you and Lucas, I thought I'd stay for awhile."

Lucas and Chester exchanged big smiles. "I never thought in a million years that it would be this boy that came back," Chester said.

Lucas nodded. "I guess the Lord works in mysterious ways."

Cru didn't know about the Lord, but it certainly seemed like fate had brought him back to the Double Diamond Ranch.

# Chapter Four

"**M**AN, IT'S HOT FOR MARCH," Dylan Matheson, the new ranch hand, voiced Penny's exact thoughts. He rose up in the saddle and pulled a bandanna out of the back pocket of his jeans, then wiped off his forehead.

He was only twenty-four, but having grown up on a ranch, he was the most experienced of the cowboys she and her father had interviewed. Maybe too experienced. Not for the first time, she wondered why a college graduate with so much potential would want to work for minimal pay. Of course, maybe he loved ranch life as much as she did and the money just wasn't as important. She could be making twice as much if she lived in a big city and used the business degree she'd gotten in college. She had tried it. But after only six months in Houston working for a marketing company, she'd had the same realization as Dorothy—there's no place like home.

Even if it was hotter than hell.

"Get used to it," she said. "The temperature will

only get higher." She pointed to the grain silo, continuing the tour of the ranch she was giving Dylan. "That's the south silo. It's where we store the grain and fill the feed trucks. But unless there's a brush fire that destroys the grazing grass, you won't have to deal with that until winter."

If Dylan stayed that long. Ranch hands came and went like the seasons. And Penny couldn't blame them. The Gardener Ranch's starting pay wasn't enough to compensate for spending long hours out in harsh winter weather, something she had pointed out to her father time and time again. Daddy refused to listen. Just like he refused to listen to other suggestions she made for improvements to the ranch. He always thought he knew best. Even when he didn't.

Maybe Evie was right. Maybe she was under her dad's thumb. But it was better than forgetting her heritage like Evie was doing. This land had been loved and cared for by generations of Gardeners. It's where she and Evie belonged. And sooner or later, Penny was going to convince her sister of that.

"Is that fence the end of your property?" Dylan asked, pulling her out of her thoughts.

She nodded. "The other side is the Double Diamond Ranch."

"Looks like the property line runs right through that creek. Who owns the water rights?"

"Both ranches have permits to use the water, but the Diamond brothers got their permit way before my father so they have seniority. Whenever there's a drought, they have rights to the water first. They don't have any cattle now, but when they did, it ticked my daddy off something fierce. Hank Gardener doesn't like being second to anyone."

Dylan laughed. "I noticed he was a little controlling in the interview."

"Controlling and arrogant and self-centered. He's like a bear with a thorn in its paw most the time."

"My grandpa was like that. Grumpy as hell and proud of it. I worked my butt off to get one word of praise from the man. He passed away a few years back from lung cancer. You know what he said to me on his death bed?"

"That he was proud of you?"

Dylan smiled. "Nope. He said, 'Boy, don't fuck up.'" He laughed. "That was my grandfather for you in a nutshell."

Penny understood perfectly. She had spent her entire life trying to get praise from a father who rarely gave it. "I think you'll be able to handle my daddy just fine. Now let's get out of this heat and go get some of Sadie's iced tea."

They headed back to the ranch. But on the way, they discovered a couple of the ranch hands searching for a missing calf. By the time they got it back with its mama, Penny was as hot as a barbecued jalapeno pepper and all she could think about was taking a swim at Mesquite Springs.

"Why don't you boys head back to the ranch and show Dylan the bunkhouse," she said. "I'll catch up with you later." She waited until Dylan had ridden off and the other hands left in a ranch dually truck before she turned her horse around and headed to the watering hole.

The cutting horse wasn't nearly as fast as Severus. But the mare was much easier to handle. All Penny had to do was tighten her legs to get Dixie to slow down as they reached the cluster of mesquite, oak, and pecan trees that surrounded the springs. She tied the mare up to a low hanging branch of a mesquite and then stripped down to her bra and panties.

The watering hole was deep enough to jump into from the rope tied to a nearby tree. The springs were freezing cold, Penny decided to wade in and let her body slowly get used to the change in temperature.

It didn't take long. After a few laps across the springs, she adjusted to the chilly water and floated on her back, closing her eyes against the sun's glare. In the relaxed state, she wasn't surprised when Cru nudged his way into her thoughts. He had been doing that a lot lately. It had been two days since he'd almost run her and Severus over, and she could only hope he was long gone by now. And yet, she couldn't help wondering why he had come back in the first place. Was it just to visit with Chester and Lucas? Or was he there for a different reason?

And why him? Why couldn't it have been one of the other boys from that summer: Logan, the dark, brooding leader of the group. Holden, the charming rich kid. Lincoln, the intense athlete. Sawyer, the jovial prankster. And Val, the sweet chubby boy with the heart of gold and a way with words. Why did it have to be Cru . . . her crush and her sister's first love?

No longer finding solace in an afternoon swim, she stood and waded to shore. She was halfway out of the water before she saw him. He was sitting on a rock tugging off his boots. He wasn't wearing a shirt and his tanned chest muscles gleamed in the late afternoon sun like loaves of bread brushed with melted butter.

She wanted to dive back in the water and shield her half-naked body, but she refused to act like an immature teenager the way she had the other day.

She defiantly lifted her chin. "You're trespassing on Gardener land."

His gaze took a slow-as-molasses trip down her body and back up to her eyes. A smile creased his handsome face. "Like father like daughter. Your daddy loved to remind me of that when I came here to swim."

"And yet here you are."

"I've never been a good listener. Especially when I want something."

The Texas twangy way he said *wont* sent a wave of heat spiraling through her. It was quickly followed by anger. "Yes, when Cru Cassidy wants something, he'll do anything to get it—no matter the consequences."

His gaze lowered to her breasts. "Sometimes the consequences are worth it."

"Especially if you aren't the one who has to pay them." As she strode over to the mesquite tree where she'd left her clothes, she tried not to think about his gaze pinned to her butt in the wet panties. She usually toweled off with her t-shirt, but today she quickly pulled it on, tugging the hem down as far as it would go.

"Why do I have the feeling that we're no longer talking about me trespassing on your land?"

She whirled at the words to find him standing only inches away. She tried to take a step back, but the prickly mesquite branches wouldn't allow it. It annoyed her to no end how breathless she suddenly felt and she had to remind herself that she wasn't a crushing thirteen-year-old girl anymore. She also had to remind herself that Evie would kill her if she let the cat out of the bag.

"What else would we be talking about?" She turned her back to him and picked up her jeans, hoping her insides would stop trembling if she didn't have to look into his mind-altering green eyes.

"You're not as funny as I remember," he said.

She buttoned her jeans before she turned around. Thankfully, he'd moved away and was sitting on the rock. "Don't act like you remember me. You didn't give me a second glance when you were fifteen."

"I remember you." He grinned. "Knock-knock."

She couldn't help but blush. "So you remember the stupid knock-knock jokes I told you. So what?"

"I remember more than the knock-knock jokes. I remember a cute redhead with braces looking at me like I hung the moon, not like I was a piece of cow dung stuck to the heel of her boot." He cocked his head. "Did I do something to hurt your feelings? I was pretty full of myself back then."

He hadn't done anything back then except be too handsome. And he still was. Which probably explained her snappish reply. "And you're not too full of yourself now?"

He cringed. "Ouch."

She pulled on her socks and boots, balancing from one foot to the other. "Sorry, but the way you drive says you haven't lost an ounce of arrogance."

"Just because I like to drive fast doesn't mean I'm an arrogant asshole."

"No, it just means that you're a careless asshole. And I don't know which one's worse."

His brow knitted. "You don't mince words, do you?"

"The truth is the truth."

He studied her for a moment before he smiled. It wasn't the practiced smile. This smile was soft and real. "You sound like Lucas. He used to say the same thing." His smile faded. "How long has he been forgetting things?"

"Since last month when he got a bad cause of the flu. I brought him some chicken noodle soup and he seemed disoriented. I was hoping it was just a fever. But even after he got better, he still kept forgetting things."

"Like his beloved recipes." Cru released his breath and stared out at the water. "He made pancakes this morning for breakfast with no flour. Although they were better than his burnt broth soup."

"He made me peanut butter cookies that tasted

like dog biscuits."

He shook his head. "If it wasn't so sad, it would be funny. But it's hard to see someone you care about losing something he loves to do." He glanced back at her. "Thank you for watching out for him and Chester. They both think the sun rises and sets on you." His gaze grew intense. "And with hair like that, it looks like it does. Penny is an appropriate name. In the sun, you sparkle like a new penny."

She self-consciously smoothed a hand over her wet hair. "Why are you here?"

"The same reason you are. I wanted to cool off."

She shook her head. "I wasn't talking about the springs. I was talking about coming back to the Double Diamond Ranch. Why would you come back to check on two old guys you only spent one summer with?"

He picked a piece of the tall grass and stuck the sweet end in his mouth as he stared out at the sun-lit water. "I don't know. Maybe because those three months were the most memorable months of my life. I learned a lot that summer."

His words surprised her. Then they made her angry. She jumped up. "If they were so memorable, why didn't you come back sooner? Why didn't you make the effort to at least check in with—?" She cut off before she said her sister's name.

He got to his feet. "You're right. I should've checked in sooner. But I'm here now. And I want to know what I can do to help."

She wanted to yell at him that he was fifteen years too late, but he wasn't talking about Evie and

Clint. He was talking about Chester and Lucas. She needed to remember that.

"You can start by convincing them they need help. A week ago, Chester went to the barn to check on his horse, Misty, and Lucas turned on the gas stove while he was gone but forgot to light it. When I got there the entire house smelled like gas. And there's no telling how many times it's happened in the past."

"I should've thought of how dangerous that old stove is. I'll order them a new one."

"I already did. I'm going to have Raul pick it up in Abilene and install it—if Chester will let him. He doesn't like to take help from people. I've tried sending the ranch hands over to fix other things, but he always runs them off. I think it has to do with the feud they have with my father."

Cru studied her. "But you don't let a feud keep you from helping two old cowboys." The intensity of his eyes made her feel fidgety . . . and hot. She felt even hotter when he reached out and smoothed a strand of wet hair away from her face. "You're a good woman, Penny Gardener."

She didn't know if it was the touch of his warm fingertips against her chilled skin or the sincere compliment that had her breath hitching and her knees turning to soft-churned butter. She swayed and Cru's hand slid around her waist to steady her. That was all it took for desire to flow and logical thought to ebb.

She couldn't think. All she could do was feel. She felt the tip of his big toe touching hers and the press of all five of his fingers against her back. She felt the flex of his forearm muscles against her side and bulge of his bicep beneath her hand. Felt the heat emanating from his naked chest and the puff of his breath against her forehead.

She wanted to break loose from the hold he had on her, but she couldn't seem to move. All she could do was stare at the beating pulse in his neck and pray that he would release her.

He didn't. Instead, he placed a finger beneath her chin and lifted it until her gaze locked with his. His eyes were a vibrant green heat that took the last of her breath away. There was no way to get it back when he lowered his head and kissed her.

As a child, she had dreamed about this kiss, dedicated pages of her diary to what it would feel like to have Cru's lips pressed against hers. As an adult, she'd learned that first kisses were like first dances—it took a while to adjust to your partner's step and pace.

But from the first touch, Penny felt like she and Cru had kissed a thousand times before. Their mouths slid together in perfect harmony and proceeded to dance a slow, sensual waltz of lips and tongues as if they'd been doing this all their lives. It was perfect. The most perfect kiss she'd ever had.

And it was wrong.

So wrong.

She pulled away. "No!"

His hands dropped immediately and he took a step back. His green eyes were confused, but he didn't voice that confusion. Instead, he gave her even more space and smiled. "Enjoy the rest of your day, Penny Gardener." He turned and headed to the springs. With her standing right there watching, he shucked off his jeans and briefs and dove into the water naked.

Penny wished she could cool off so easily. Unfortunately, she was afraid nothing would douse the fire Cru Cassidy's kiss had lit inside her.

# CHAPTER FIVE

CRU DIDN'T LIKE ROUTINE. GROWING up in a Catholic orphanage had been enough to sour him on monotonous schedules and repetitive rituals. After he graduated from high school and set out on his own, he vowed to do what he wanted when he wanted and fly by the seat of his pants. He chose jobs that worked on commission so he could set his own hours and quit when the urge hit him. Never signed an apartment lease for longer than three months at a time. And didn't make plans more than a week in advance.

But at the Double Diamond Ranch he slipped into a routine without even knowing it. He woke up at the crack of dawn and made coffee—mostly because he didn't want Chester making the black crud he liked to drink—then he showered and shaved before helping Lucas with breakfast. He'd learned if he handed Lucas the ingredients, the old guy didn't seem to make as many mistakes. Once breakfast was over, he cleaned up the dishes and then went out to take care of Misty. The old horse was as ornery as Chester and Lucas and had given Cru a nip or two before she got to know him. But once she did, she greeted him every morning and evening with a cheerful nicker. Probably because he always brought her a treat. It wasn't long before they'd formed a bond. Maybe after he finished seeing the world, Cru would get himself a dog. There was something calming about being around animals.

Once he finished taking care of Misty in the mornings, he worked on one of the numerous things that needed to be fixed around the ranch. He'd never been much of a handyman. He'd always lived in apartments where the managers took care of broken toilets or dripping faucets. And at the St. James's Home for Children, Sister Stella had done all the handiwork. Once, she'd tried to teach him, but he hadn't been interested.

Now he wished he had paid more attention. He easily fixed the clogged bathtub drain with drain cleaner and the squeaky back door hinges with some spray oil. But the broken toilet in the main bathroom was a little more complicated. Once he had the lid off the tank, he didn't have a clue what to do. Lucas tried to give him instructions, but his memory of toilet fixing was as bad as his memory of recipes. And Chester had always preferred ranch work to housework. So Cru had to rely on the Internet. After watching a YouTube video, he thought he had it figured out and headed into town to the hardware store to get what he needed. But the big guy behind the counter had him second-guessing his Internet knowledge.

"The thing about running toilets is that it could be a lot of different things causing them to run." He leaned his muscular forearms on the counter. "It could be the flapper, or the flapper chain, or the overflow valve, or a leaky fill valve, or even a corroded toilet handle. That was what it turned out to be on Floyd Herman's toilet. Of course, he didn't find that out until he'd fixed all the other things. Does the handle look corroded?"

Cru shrugged. "To be honest, I didn't really look at the handle. But there is a crack in the flapper thingy."

The man nodded thoughtfully. "Of course, if the flapper is old enough to have a crack in it, the overflow valve and fill valve could too. Especially when Lucas hasn't been in for toilet parts in a good six years." Cru was impressed he kept such close tabs on his customers' toilets. Although the pretty blonde who came hustling down an aisle seemed to keep closer tabs.

"More like seven." She held out a hand. "Emma Johansen. And this yammering fool is my business partner, Boone Murphy."

Cru took her hand. "Cru Cassidy."

Her eyes narrowed as she gave his hand a firm shake. "Cru Cassidy? Why does that name sound familiar?"

"I spent a summer out at the Double Diamond Ranch when I was a teenager."

A sassy smile flirted with her lips. "So you're one of those bad boys my mama warned me about."

Cru laughed. "I'm one of those boys." He winked at her. "Although now I'm only bad on occasion."

One blond eyebrow arched. "Somehow, I doubt that." She handed him a toilet repair kit. "Since you don't know what's wrong with your toilet, you should just buy this entire set now and be done with it. If you don't need everything, I'm sure you'll need it for one of the other two toilets out at the ranch. Extra toilet parts always come in handy. And this kit happens to be on special this week so you might want to get two."

"Thank you, Ms. Johansen. That sounds like good advice."

"You're welcome. And just call me Emma."

He flashed a smile. "Thank you, Emma."

"No problem at all." She scowled at Boone. "Some people just like to talk folks to death instead of giving them what they need."

Boone straightened. "I was getting around to getting him what he needed when you butted in."

"And maybe by next Christmas he would've gotten something to fix his toilet." She shook her head. "I swear I don't know why your father gave you his half of the hardware store when you don't know a screw from a nut."

Boone stared at her. "Oh, I know a nut when I see one. And I don't know why your father gave you his half of the store when you have no business sense. You can't balance our accounts to save your soul and would give away the entire inventory if I weren't here to keep an eye on you. That repair kit"—he pointed to the package in Cru's hand—

"isn't on special. You just put it on special because you think Cru here is cute and you're looking to trap a husband."

Emma's eyes widened and her mouth dropped open for a second before she grabbed a package of plastic tubing and hurled it at Boone. He ducked just in time and the tubing bounced off the wall of tools behind the counter. "You jerk!" she yelled. "How dare you embarrass me—" She cut off when the bell over the door jangled. Cru was thankful for the timely interruption. He was even more thankful when Penny Gardener stepped in.

He hadn't seen her since Mesquite Springs, but not from lack of trying. He'd gotten her phone number from Chester and called her numerous times, but she never answered or returned his messages. So he'd stopped by the Gardener Ranch. She hadn't been there, and the interrogation he'd gotten from the housekeeper had dissuaded him from going back again. If not for the kiss, he might have thought she wasn't interested in him. But there was no way a woman could kiss him like she wanted to crawl inside his skin and not be interested. Which meant she was just playing hard to get.

And Cru had always enjoyed a good game of chase.

"Well, hey there, Miss Penny," he said in a slow drawl.

She visibly bristled. If she'd been a cat, there was little doubt he'd have gotten a scratch right across his nose. He grinned. He didn't mind getting scratched up a little either.

"Hey, Pen," Emma said. "I haven't seen you in town for a while."

Penny pulled her gaze away from Cru and smiled at Emma. "Hey, Emma. How's your daddy's gout doin'?"

"It comes and goes. Mama has him on a strict diet, but he cheats every chance he gets."

Penny laughed. The sight of her flashing white teeth and sparkling eyes made Cru's knees weak. "Sadie's been trying to put my daddy on a low-cholesterol diet for years." She glanced at Cru and her laughter died. "Arrogant men just don't like being told no."

Emma glanced at Boone. "Amen, sister. So are you here in town to add your suggestion for a new name for Simple in the pot?"

"No, I needed some barbed staples to fix a fence. And I'm not coming up with a new name. I like the name Simple."

"So do I." Boone pointed to a sign on the wall behind the cash register that said "Keep Simple Simple." "The only reason Mayor Landers wants to change it is because that newspaper reporter referred to her as a Simpleton."

Cru had to laugh. In the big cities he'd lived in, the news was filled with shootings, deadly car accidents, and hate crimes. Here, the big news was changing the town name.

"I like Simple," he said. "Nothing wrong with things being simpler."

Penny sent him an annoyed look. "Too bad you can't vote in November. Voting is for residents only and I'm sure you'll be leaving town soon."

He grinned. "Wishful thinking?"

She ignored him and looked at Emma. "I better get those staples and get back to the ranch. Those fences aren't going to fix themselves."

Boone hurried around the counter. "I'll be happy to help you, Penny. We just happen to have those on special."

Emma rolled her eyes at Cru as the two disappeared down an aisle. "Talk about me giving away the store for a pretty face." She moved behind the counter. "Sorry about the ruckus earlier. Our fathers were best friends and business partners. Unfortunately, Boone and I don't get along so well. Probably because we're only children and were raised together like siblings." She took the toilet repair kit from him and scanned it. "You have siblings?"

It was a good question. One he couldn't answer. When he was a kid, he'd spent a lot of time thinking about the woman who had given birth to him and wondering if she had given birth to other children—children she had kept or, like him, deserted in the bathroom of a bus station. But those thoughts had only led to depression so he'd stopped wondering and started thinking of himself as a single entity. No mother or father. No siblings. Just a lone helium balloon drifting through the skies, not tethered to anyone or anything. Or, at least, he had until he'd gone to Father Stephen's funeral and Sister Bernadette had given him the letter.

He pushed the thoughts of Father Stephen's

passing and the letter from his mind and took out his wallet. "No. No siblings."

Emma sighed. "Lucky."

After he paid for the toilet repair kit, he thanked Emma and headed outside. He could've gone back to the ranch, but he didn't. Instead, he tossed the bag in the passenger seat of his Porsche and then walked back to the Gardener Ranch truck parked right in front of the hardware store. While he was waiting for Penny to come out, he glanced around the town.

It had changed very little in fifteen years. Some of the businesses were different, but the old brick-faced buildings that lined the main street were the same. According to Chester and Lucas, the town was founded in the eighteen hundreds by settlers looking for prosperity in the west. Since the ground was so rocky, cattle seemed to be the best choice for a livelihood and soon ranches popped up all over the area. And when the nearby Chisholm Trail was established, it made getting the cattle to the Kansas railways for shipping much easier.

Cru would bet it had been one rowdy cow town back then. Now it was a peaceful town with ordinary folks going about their daily business. Although the woman with the spiky blue hair and purple-framed glasses walking toward him didn't look so ordinary.

"You the new ranch hand Hank Gardener hired?" she asked in a thick Texas accent.

He took off his cowboy hat. "No, ma'am. I'm staying out at the Double Diamond."

Her eyebrows lifted. "Well, it's about damn time those two hired someone to help them. The entire town has been worried sick about them living out there all alone. I've stopped by a few times to see if they needed anything, but they don't much care for company."

Cru laughed. "That's putting it mildly. Did Chester run you off with his shotgun?"

She grinned. "No. Just a few cuss words." She held out a hand. "Raynelle Coffman."

He shook her hand. "Cru Cassidy. Nice to meet you." He glanced down at her purple t-shirt with Simple Market written across it. "You work at the grocery store?"

"For close to thirteen years."

He feigned surprise. "You must've started when you were ten."

She swatted his arm. "Well, ain't you the charmer. But I started working there right after my husband left me and I had to feed my two kids. They're grown now. Suzette just got married and is living in Galveston. And Brandon is . . . pretty much a bum. But most of that is my fault for not kicking him out of the house sooner. It's hard to let go of your baby boy."

For good moms, maybe. For bad ones, it was as easy as walking away.

"Would you look at me babbling on?" Raynelle said. "I'm probably boring you to tears."

"Not at all." He winked at her. "I've always liked a woman who can keep up a conversation."

She laughed and swatted him again. "Well, I can

sure do that. Now I better get back to work. You come into the market and see me any time, Cru Cassidy."

"Will do. You have a good day, Raynelle." As he watched her head down the street, the door of the hardware store opened and Penny stepped out. She didn't look happy to see him. If she was playing hard-to-get, she was going a little overboard.

She strode toward him. "Would you stop stalking me?"

"Stalking you? I wasn't the one who followed you to Mesquite Springs and into town."

"I did not follow you here! I came here for barb-wire nails. And how could I follow you to Mesquite Springs when I was there first?"

God, she was breathtaking when she was angry. Her fiery hair was pulled back in a low, messy ponytail with straggly strands framing a face without one brushstroke of makeup to cover the flushed cheeks or multitude of freckles. He'd never thought a fresh-faced girl-next-door type would flame his passion, but the need to smooth those messy strands away from her face, cradle her chin in his palm, and kiss every one of those freckles was so strong he had to fist his hand.

"You weren't at Mesquite Springs first," he said.

"You hid in the trees and watched me undress?"

"I wasn't spying. I was standing in the shade of the trees taking off my shirt." He lifted an eyebrow. "Unlike you, who purposely hid so you could spy on me and Logan swimming at the springs." Her face turned bright red, and he laughed. Which seemed to make her even madder.

She glanced around to see if anyone was around and hissed under her breath. "I was just a naïve kid!"

"Who followed two boys to Mesquite Springs in hopes of getting an eyeful. Was that what you were hoping for when you followed me there the other day?" he teased. "If you want to go skinny dipping with me, honey, all you have to do is ask."

Her mouth dropped open before she snapped it shut. "You're the last man I'd follow anywhere." She headed for the driver's side of her truck.

Cru should cut his losses and let her go. This game of hard to get *was* starting to make him feel like a stalker. And yet, he couldn't seem to forget the kiss. He'd kissed lots of women in his life, but not one had melted in his arms like a pat of butter snuggled between two hot cakes. He wanted to make her melt again. Dammit, he was going to make her melt again.

He followed her. "Look, I was only teasing you about spying on me and Logan. I didn't mean to make you mad."

She stopped at her door and turned to him. "I'm not mad."

"I don't know what you'd call it. You've been treating me like a burr under your saddle since I almost ran you over." He squinted at her. "Is that why you're ticked at me? Or does it have more to do with the kiss?"

She glanced around. "Would you lower your voice?"

"Why? Do you have a boyfriend lurking around you don't want knowing you kissed me out at Mesquite Springs?"

"Yes, I have a boyfriend." He might've been annoyed if he hadn't read the lie in her eyes. Penny's eyes were like a clear blue lake. Nothing could hide in them.

"Really? Who?"

"You just met him in the hardware store."

"Boone would certainly like to be your boyfriend, but he's not."

"And how do you know?"

He brushed a strand of hair back from her cheek and smiled when her lips parted and her breath rushed out in a startled exhalation. "It's called chemistry, Sweetness. You and Boone have none." He stroked a finger down her stubborn jawline to the soft skin beneath her chin. "You and I, on the other hand, have it in spades."

She inhaled a quivery breath and kept her gaze lowered. "I don't know what you're talking about."

"Yes, you do. You know exactly what I'm talking about. But for some reason that I can't figure out, you're fighting it." He lifted her chin with his finger until her gaze met his. Her eyes said it all. She felt it. She felt the same deep pull of attraction he felt. He read the passion steeping in her baby blues. He could also read the fear. And he understood it. He felt a little scared himself. He'd been attracted to women before, but never with this intensity. Never with this all-consuming need.

Using just his finger, he drew her closer. "You

can't fight chemistry, Sweet Pen. All you can do is surrender." He dipped his head under the brim of her cowboy hat and kissed her.

With the way she'd been acting, he expected some kind of hesitation. Instead, as soon as his lips touched hers, she opened like a flower to a bee. He couldn't stop himself from sliding his tongue in and gathering all the warm, sweet nectar being offered. She tasted like sweet tea spiked with the finest scotch whiskey—intoxicating fire all wrapped up in pure innocence. And he couldn't get enough. He cradled her jaw and pressed the hand still holding his hat against her back, bringing her flush against him.

She released a low moan and he felt it all the way to the toes of his boots as she wrapped her arms around his neck. Her fingernails scraped through the hair at the base of his neck as she deepened the pull of her lips and the sensuous strokes of her tongue. She had him hot, hard, and ready in about two seconds flat. But unless he wanted to give the townsfolk something to gossip about over supper, he needed to bring a stop to things.

With a nip on her lower lip, he eased back from the kiss and whispered in a voice hoarse with desire, "Let's get out of here." Completely ignoring him, she pulled him in for another lip-searing kiss. It took a lot of willpower to end it and put some much needed breathing room between them. "Damn," he said. "I can't think straight around you. And unless we want to start a scandal, honey, we need to move this party elsewhere. I'd suggest my place, but I can't see Chester and Lucas being over-joyed if I had my way with you in the spare room."

She stared at him in confusion. "Have your way with me?"

"Or you can have your way with me." He winked. "I don't mind you being in charge."

The desire completely drained from her eyes, leaving that disgusted look he didn't care for. "No one is having their way with anyone."

Dammit, not this again.

He tugged on his cowboy hat. "Okay, I'm not quite understanding all the rules of this game we're playing. I don't mind a little hard to get, but this back and forth business is giving me whiplash. It's pretty obvious you want me. And I want you. Since we're two single consenting adults, I don't see the problem. Why shouldn't we enjoy each other's company while I'm here?"

The sudden storminess of her eyes warned him what was coming next. The punch she delivered to his stomach had him sucking wind and staggering back against the car parked next to hers.

"What the hell?" he gasped.

She glared at him. "Sorry, but you already screwed over one Gardener sister. You're not going to screw over this one." She hopped into her truck and backed out, almost running over his toes in the process, then took off in a squeal of tires.

Cru stood there holding his stomach and trying to figure out what had happened. Her sister? How had he screwed over her sister?

Like a bolt of lightning from heaven, the answer

hit him. And he could've kicked himself for not thinking of it before.

A man can never try to get lucky with two sisters.

# CHAPTER SIX

IT WAS A LITTLE AFTER three o'clock when Penny finally got to Evie's house in Abilene. Evie was still at work, so Penny let herself in the back door using the spare key under the mat. Once in the kitchen, she opened the refrigerator to get something to drink. When she saw the package of ham, she realized she was hungry. Which was surprising since she never thought she'd be able to eat again after what she'd done.

She'd kissed Cru Cassidy. Twice. The first kiss she could pass off as Cru catching her off-guard. The second kiss couldn't be passed off as anything but pure unadulterated desire. She wanted Cru. She didn't want to want him, but she couldn't help it. And it had nothing to do with her childhood crush. At thirteen, she'd dreamed about innocent kisses. After the kiss today, she couldn't stop thinking about hot, nasty sex.

She now understood why Evie had fallen into bed with him so easily. His kisses were mind-altering and his charm hard to resist. But Penny would resist. Cru had broken her sister's heart and she would never forgive him for that. While Penny had been upset when Cru left that summer, Evie had been devastated. Penny hadn't completely understood her sister's depression until she found out about the baby. Then her sister's sadness after all the Double Diamond boys had left made sense. Cru hadn't just stolen a few kisses. He'd stolen her sister's heart.

The sound of the front door opening startled her out of her thoughts. Sneakers thumped against the wood floor in the living room and she figured that Clint was home from school.

"I told you that I can't hang out today, Tommy. I have homework to do."

"So do it later," Tommy said. "Shit, I wish your mom drank. After the geometry test, I could sure use a shot of tequila. I tried to cheat off Daryl Bixby, but the geek caught me and covered his paper. Hey, why don't we head over to my house? My dad always keeps a six-pack in the garage refrigerator."

"I have to be here when my mom calls or I'll be in big trouble. And don't you dare light up. My mom with kill me if she smells cigarette smoke."

"Hey, give me that back. The smell will be gone by the time she gets home. She didn't smell it last time, did she?"

Penny stepped out of the kitchen to find Tommy sprawled out on the couch in the living room and Clint holding a cigarette. "You're right. She probably won't know you were smoking in her house. But now I do."

Tommy quickly jumped up from the couch and grabbed his backpack. "Oh hey, Miss Gardener. I just stopped by to do homework with Clint. But since you're here, I probably better get home."

"So you can get drunk on your daddy's beer?"

"N–No, ma'am. I was just kiddin' about that. See you, Clint." He hurried out the door.

When he was gone, Penny walked over and took the cigarette from Clint's hand. "I see how you ended up with Saturday detention. You're lucky you didn't get suspended." She stuffed the cigarette in her back pocket so Evie wouldn't find it in the trash and go ballistic. "That guy is a complete loser. You know that, right?"

"Tommy isn't that bad. He's just going through some crap right now after his parents got a divorce."

"I'd accept that excuse if his parents had just gotten a divorce. But they've been divorced for over a year, Clint. Which means that he's just gotten in the habit of using that as an excuse for his bad behavior." She tipped her head. "Just like you use Tommy as an excuse for yours so you don't disappoint your mother. You know right from wrong."

Clint shrugged. "Sometimes things don't always fit neatly into right or wrong holes, Aunt Pen. Sometimes the line gets blurred."

She knew exactly what he was talking about. Cru's lips were extremely good at blurring lines. But she knew right from wrong. And kissing Cru had been wrong. Totally wrong.

She hooked her arm through Clint's. "Come on. I'll make you a sandwich."

They sat at the breakfast bar and ate their ham and cheese sandwiches. After being reminded about what a mistake she'd made with Cru, Penny had lost her appetite and only nibbled on hers while Clint devoured his in just a few bites.

"You're a human garbage disposal," she said with a smile.

"I'm a growing boy." He finished off his sandwich, then reached for hers.

"Hey!" She swatted his hand. "That's mine."

He stuck out his bottom lip. "You wouldn't deny your favorite nephew food, would you?"

"You're my only nephew. I'm sure, one day, your mama will have another son that I'll like much better."

She thought he would laugh, but instead he grew serious and looked down at his empty plate. "She's thinking about marrying Edward."

"I heard. How do you feel about that?"

Most boys would be upset about getting a stepdad, but Clint wasn't most boys. He was a kid who loved his mom and wanted what was best for her. "Okay, I guess. I mean he's nice to Mom and it will be good for her to have someone when I leave for college."

She slid her sandwich over to him. "You'll always be my favorite nephew."

He grinned. "Knew it." He polished off her sandwich and followed it with an entire bag of nacho-flavored Doritos. As he munched on the chips and talked about school, she couldn't help examining his features. She didn't find any similarities to Cru. Clint looked like a younger version of her daddy—something that Evie refused to acknowledge—except with dark brown eyes with golden splashes in the irises.

When her father had learned Evie was pregnant, he'd wanted her to put the baby up for adoption. He'd made all the arrangements and sent Evie to Dallas when she first started to show. Evie had been a scared fifteen-year-old and had gone along with her father's wishes. But all it had taken was Evie holding Clint one time for her to change her mind. Penny was so glad she had. She didn't want to think about what life would be like without her sweet nephew.

"Do I have a booger hanging out of my nose, Aunt Pen?" Clint asked. "Why do you keep staring at me?"

"Sorry. It's just been a while since I've seen that cute face." She pinched his cheek. "Now get your homework done so your mom won't yell at both of us when she gets home from work. While you're working on it, I'll figure out something to make for dinner."

"I wish you'd let Mom make dinner. I still puke in my mouth when I think of your pork tacos."

She jumped up from her barstool. "Oh, you're going to pay with noogies for that, Mister."

She soon figured out that it was a mistake to try and wrangle with her nephew now that he was bigger that she was. She might be a strong cowgirl from all the ranch work she did, but Clint was like a big lab puppy who didn't know his own strength.

She ended up being the one in the headlock getting hard noogies. She had to reach up and tickle
his armpit to get him to release her.

"Hey, no fair," he said.

She grinned. "Everything's fair in war, baby boy."

It turned out Clint was right about her cooking skills. The spaghetti she made was mushy and
the sauce so garlicky she ended up tossing both
out and ordering pizza delivery. But Evie didn't
seem to care about what was for dinner when she
walked through the door and saw Penny.

"Pen!" She pulled her into a tight hug. "What
are you doing here during the week?" She drew
back with concerned eyes. "Is everything okay at
the ranch?"

She pinned on a smile. "Everything's fine. Can't
a girl miss her nephew and sis? Now stop being
a worrywart and let's eat the pizza before it gets
cold."

"Amen," Clint said. "I'm starving."

During dinner, Clint wasn't as talkative about
school with his mother as he had been with Penny.
When Evie asked if he'd stayed away from Tommy
that day, he shot a quick glance over at Penny
before he vaguely answered. "He wanted to hang
out after school, but I told him I had homework."

Penny could've mentioned Tommy being there
and the cigarette and alcohol. But since Clint had
tried to get rid of Tommy, she kept her mouth shut.
Obviously, her line between right and wrong was
totally blurred.

After dinner, Clint headed to his room to play

video games. Once he was gone, Evie got up from her chair and opened the broom closet. Penny was surprised when she pulled out the mop bucket.

"I get that you love to clean, Evie. But can you wait until I leave?"

"I'm not planning on mopping." She pulled a bottle of wine out of the bucket.

Penny laughed. "That's not exactly a great hiding place."

"It is when your son hates to clean as much as Clint does. His room looks like a tornado hit it . . . twice." Evie opened the bottle of wine and then took two wine glasses from the cupboard. "Let's go out to the patio."

Once they were sitting on the patio with a glass of merlot, Evie looked at her. "So what's going on? And don't tell me it's nothing. I can tell by your face that something happened. Is it Daddy? Did you get in a fight? Or is it Lucas? Has his sprained ankle gotten worse?"

"I haven't seen Lucas in a while." She took a deep drink of wine and then wrinkled her nose. "Dang, I don't know how you drink this stuff." She set the glass down on the table.

Evie laughed. "Sorry, but six-packs of Bud are harder to hide. Now quit hedging and get to the reason you're here."

She swallowed hard. "Cru Cassidy is still at Lucas and Chester's. I guess he's been helping them."

Evie causally took a sip of her wine and shrugged. "Good for him. Maybe he's not such a bad boy after all."

Penny couldn't keep Evie's secret a second more. She leaned up and rested her forearms on the table. "Don't you care that the father of your child has come back to Simple?"

Evie choked on her wine and Penny reached over and thumped her back until she caught her breath. "Who told you that?"

"No one had to tell me. He's the only logical choice. Are you saying it was another Double Diamond boy?"

Evie fiddled with the stem of her glass. "I'm not telling you who Clint's father is."

"Why not? I realize why you didn't tell me when I was thirteen and couldn't keep a secret to save my soul. But I can keep a secret now."

"It's not so much about you keeping the secret. I just don't want you to have to feel guilty about lying to Daddy, Clint, and the entire town. Believe me, I feel guilty enough."

"Then why don't you tell the truth, Evie? If not to Daddy and the town, then at least to Clint? I think he's old enough to handle it."

Evie blew out a breath. "You're probably right. The other night he started questioning the story I gave him about his father."

Penny rolled her eyes. "Anyone with half a brain would question the ridiculous story that his dad is a foreign exchange student you had one night of passion with before he headed back to Spain."

Evie looked thoroughly offended. "It's not a ridiculous story. I did date that cute foreign exchange student from Spain. And Daddy and the entire town of Simple believes Fernando was the one who got me pregnant."

"Because it's much easier to blame a foreigner than someone from their beloved Texas. But Clint isn't as gullible. If he's asking, you know it's only a matter of time before he Googles Fernando and tries to contact him. The poor guy won't know what's going on if he should get an email from some American teenager claiming to be his son."

"Fine. I'll tell him, but I'm waiting until he gets through this belligerent teenage stage he's going through. He already hates me enough as is. I don't want him hating me any more."

"Clint doesn't hate you." Penny reached across the table and squeezed her sister's hand. "He loves you, Evie. He'll forgive you. And I'll be right there to make sure he understands how hard it was for a sixteen-year-old girl to become a mother and how scared you were of Daddy finding out it was a Double Diamond boy and doing something in retaliation." She paused. "Do you still love . . . Clint's father?"

Evie lifted her glass and stared down at her wine. "Your first love is hard to forget. Especially when he's your son's father." She glanced up. "So that's the only reason you came? You just wanted to tell me Cru Cassidy was still at Chester and Lucas's?"

Penny should tell her about the kiss. There was little doubt that someone in Simple had witnessed it and the gossip was already spreading like wildfire. But how did you go about telling your sister you'd kissed her first love—not once, but twice? Before she could find the words, Evie spoke.

"Edward wants to get married in Cancun this fall and I'm thinking about saying 'yes.'"

Penny forgot about the kiss and stared at her sister. "This fall?" When Evie had mentioned Edward's proposals, Penny had assumed she'd have a good year to talk her sister out of it. But fall was less than six months away. And if Evie married Edward, she'd never come home. Edward wasn't the small town type. He was the vice-president of a bank and loved his job and the prestige that went with it.

"But you can't get married," she said before she remembered her sister was exactly like their father and hated being told what to do. "I mean you can't get married in Cancun. You're terrified of flying."

"I'm not terrified. I just have a little anxiety."

"A little? That's not what I would call the major panic attacks you have. The flight crews and passengers are probably still talking about your complete meltdowns."

"I'm not that bad. Besides, I'm not going to fly to Cancun. We're driving to Florida and taking a cruise."

"But you don't love him, Evie."

"And he knows that. He did the entire love thing with his first marriage and it turned out badly. He's ready to have a marriage based on friendship and mutual interests. We have a lot in common."

"Like what?"

"We both work at the bank. We both have sons who will soon go away to college. And I think we're both worried about being lonely."

"Loneliness is not a good reason to get married. If you moved back to the ranch, you wouldn't have to be lonely either. You'd have an entire town filled with people who would want to hang out with you. And me and Daddy." Evie got an annoyed look on her face and Penny realized she wasn't going to sway her by mentioning Daddy. "Fine, but you can't get married in Cancun. What about all your friends and family who will want to attend the wedding?"

"They'll all be invited."

"You know that most folks in Simple can't afford an expensive trip like that." It was a bald-faced lie. Most of the townsfolk would jump at an excuse to vacation in Cancun. She threw down her trump card. "Besides, you have to get married at the ranch. You know Mama wanted both us girls to be married beneath the same rose arbor she and Daddy were married under."

Evie's eyes misted over. "I forgot about Mama's arbor." She sighed. "I'll talk to Edward and see if he minds getting married at the ranch in the fall and going to Cancun for our honeymoon."

"What about the spring? That will give you more time to plan." And Penny more time to stop it. "You know how you love to plan, Evie."

Before Evie could reply, the sliding glass door opened and Clint peeked his head out. "Your phone keeps ringing, Aunt Pen."

"It's probably Daddy. I forgot to call and tell him that I was coming to see you."

Evie snorted. "And you say you're not under his

thumb."

"I'm not." She pushed back her chair and got up. "But he'll be worried if I don't call him back."

Her father did sound worried. "Where are you?" he asked as soon as he answered the phone.

"I'm visiting Evie."

He released his breath. "Thank God."

His relief worried her. "What's going on, Daddy? Did something happen at the ranch?"

"Not at our ranch. But I just got word the Double Diamond is on fire."

# CHAPTER SEVEN

"I AIN'T STAYIN' AT NO HOSPITAL so they can prod and poke me like some diseased calf."

"They aren't going to treat you like a diseased calf," Cru snapped. He was usually a pretty patient guy, but he was exhausted and the stitches in his shoulder hurt like hell. He was completely out of patience for two old guys who wouldn't listen to reason. "You're going to take the doctor's advice and stay the night."

"Like hell I am." Chester waved a hand. "Move out of the way, boy, so I can get up from this damned uncomfortable bed and go check on Lucas."

"Your brother is fine, Mr. Diamond." The doctor spoke to Chester in a much calmer voice than Cru had. "If you don't want to stay, I certainly can't force you. But you have to know that this is against my recommendation. You might not have any external injures from the explosion, but until we run tests, we won't know about internal injuries."

"My innards are just fine." Chester sat up on the

bed. "Now what did you do with Lucas?"

The doctor shook his head in defeat. "He's down the hall getting fitted with a boot for his sprained ankle."

Chester snorted and whispered to Cru loud enough for the doctor to hear. "That shows you who we're dealing with here. Who puts a boot on a man with a sprained ankle? Now let's go get Lucas and go home."

"We can't go home, Chester," Cru said. "Are you forgetting about what happened to the house?"

Chester scowled. "I'm not senile. I know exactly what happened. Lucas turned on the stove then forgot to light it and blew the kitchen to smithereens."

That was exactly what had happened. And as it had been doing all night, Cru's stomach tightened sickeningly with the thought that all three of them could have been blown to smithereens right along with the kitchen. It was a miracle they hadn't been.

Cru had always believed in God. Growing up in a Catholic orphanage, it was pretty much a given. But he'd viewed God as an old white-haired guy who sat on a cloud in heaven and laughed as He watched the antics of the humans He'd created. Cru had never thought of Him as a God who got too involved in day-to-day life. But he started to rethink this belief after he, Chester, and Lucas survived the gas explosion that burned down the house.

It had been close to seven o'clock when Misty had started raising a ruckus in the barn. Cru had gotten up to go check on her and Chester had insisted on going with him. When they got there, they couldn't find any reason for the horse to be upset. They checked Misty over, then looked around the barn for a skunk or squirrel that might've wandered in. After finding nothing that would've spooked the horse, they'd headed back to the house and run into Lucas.

"Did one of you yahoos move my bag of popcorn? I looked in the freezer, but it's not there."

Chester had snorted. "You don't store popcorn in the freezer, you old—" Before he could say coot, the night had lit up. The blast knocked Lucas into Cru's arms. He'd turned to shelter both Lucas and Chester from flying debris and a shard of glass had struck him in the shoulder. But other than that, no one had been harmed. All because Misty had decided to throw a fit for no apparent reason and Lucas couldn't find his popcorn. Of course, it would've been better if God had reminded Lucas to light the gas stove after turning it on. Or even kept the water heater from lighting and igniting the gas that had filled the kitchen. Then Chester and Lucas would still have their home.

"We can't go back to a house that's blown to smithereens," Cru said. "We'll have to stay in a hotel until you can figure out what you want to do. So you might as well stay here a night."

"We can sleep in the barn. It won't be the first time I've slept in one."

"You're not sleeping in a barn." A woman stepped into the room. A pretty blond woman who looked vaguely familiar. Before Cru could place her, Chester helped him out.

"Evie!" He held out his arms and Evie walked straight into them and gave him a tight hug.

It looked like Evie had grown up. She still had a phenomenal body, but she wasn't as beautiful as Cru remembered. Her hair was an ordinary blond—nothing like a fiery sunset of strawberry blond and reds. And she had no sun-kissed cheeks or sprinkling of freckles.

Now that he knew why Penny had been avoiding him, he planned to put his attraction to her behind him and move on. But for some reason, he couldn't stop thinking about her and the kisses they'd shared. He'd never particularly cared for kissing. To him, it was just a means to an end. But with Penny, kissing was almost as good as the main event. He loved the way she felt in his arms and the way she tasted on his tongue and the way she followed every slow sip and deep slide. And damned if he didn't wish he hadn't been so boob crazy as a kid and gone after Evie. But it was too late for wishes. He'd already burned his bridges.

Evie drew back from Chester. "Are you okay? Penny and I have been so worried about you."

"Fit as a fiddle. It will take more than a little fire to get rid of this ornery old cowboy."

Evie laughed. "Thank God for that. Although I wish we had known before we left Abilene. Penny drove like a maniac getting here. Even I had trouble following her and I've always had a lead foot."

"Where is Penny?" Cru asked.

She glanced over at him. She didn't look surprised to see him. Penny must've told her he was there. He couldn't help wondering if she'd told her about the kisses they'd shared. If she had, Evie didn't seem mad about it. Her tone held no emotions whatsoever. "Hey, Cru."

Looking into her blue eyes, he thought he'd feel something—some leftover attraction from that summer so long ago. But all he felt was a slight amount of nostalgia.

"Hey, Evie. You grew up."

"So did you. What happened to the scrawny boy who thought he was God's gift to women?"

"Scrawny? And here I thought you'd been so impressed with my concave chest and non-existent biceps."

Her blue eyes sparkled with humor. "Which is why you kept taking off your shirt."

He laughed. "I did use any excuse to whip my shirt off and strut my stuff, didn't I? Unlike Logan, who refused to take his shirt off for anything. Hell, he even swam in his t-shirt."

Her smile faded as if he'd snuffed it out with a strong exhalation and she changed the subject. "Penny's with Lucas. When I left he was giving an orderly a hard time about having to sit in a wheelchair." She glanced at the doctor. "I'm going to make a bet that you've been getting the same treatment here."

The doctor nodded. "I'd like both Mr. Diamond and his brother to stay overnight so I can run some tests, but I don't think that's going to happen."

"They'll stay overnight." Penny wheeled Lucas into the room.

Cru didn't know why he suddenly felt relieved. He tried to tell himself it had to do with her taking over some of the responsibility for Chester and Lucas, but deep down he knew there was more to it than that. There was something about her big blue eyes filled with such worry and concern that made him want to pull her into his arms. And what scared him was he didn't know if it was to comfort her or himself.

The doctor didn't wait for Chester and Lucas to argue before he quickly headed for the door. "I'll take care of getting a room."

Once he was gone, Penny looked at Cru. "It's all my fault. If I'd had Raul pick up the stove sooner, this never would've happened."

The tears that shimmered in her eyes gutted Cru. "It's not your fault. It's mine. I was the one who should've been keeping an eye on things. I took over the cooking and warned Lucas about using the stove, but I should've known he couldn't stay out of the kitchen."

"Why would I stay out of my own damned kitchen?" Lucas said. "And I swear I lit the stove."

"Then how did our kitchen blow up, you old coot?" Chester asked.

Lucas looked totally bewildered and his age-spotted hands started to shake. "I'm the reason our house burned down?"

Before Cru could step in and calm him, Chester did. "It ain't a big thing, Lucas. We've lived through worse." He grinned. "Remember when that bull almost stomped me to death? Or when that little señorita's daddy filled your butt with buckshot when he found you sneaking out her window?"

Chester could usually tease Lucas out of a sad mood. But not this time. This time, he didn't crack a smile. "But I blew up our home. I took away everything we own in this world. All because I was too mule-headed to accept that I don't remember as good as I used to and should stay the hell out of the kitchen." A tear trickled down his weathered cheek. It was too much for Cru. He knelt in front of the wheelchair and took Lucas's hand.

"Chester is right. It's not a big deal. Once you get the insurance money, you'll be able to build a brand new house. Or maybe you'll decide you want to use the money to head to Florida to a nice retirement community with no gas stoves or acres of land to have to deal with."

The look Lucas and Chester exchanged said that wasn't going to happen.

"We ain't goin' to Florida," Chester said. "We're Texas born and raised and this is where we'll die. And about that insurance, we don't have any. The company upped our premium so much last year, we figured we could do without it. I guess we was wrong."

Cru really wanted to yell in frustration at the two stubborn fools. And Evie and Penny looked like they wanted to do the same. Instead, they all just remained speechless until the doctor and an orderly with another wheelchair came back in.

"Mr. and Mr. Diamond's room is ready," the doctor said.

"We don't need no room," Lucas said. "Just like I don't need this contraption." He lifted his foot with the black orthopedic boot. "It's pure foolishness, is what it is. As were all those questions you asked me when I got here. What's the date? What time is it? And do I know where I am? Of course, I know where I am. I'm in a damned hospital much too late."

The doctor bit back a smile. "You're right. But can you tell me the exact date?" When Lucas looked confused, the doctor asked other questions. Lucas could answer some, but not all. Which had him getting angry.

"I ain't got that alls-heimers if that's what you're thinkin'." He sounded mad, but it was easy to read the fear in his eyes.

The doctor must've read it too because he spoke in a gentle voice. "There are other reasons for memory loss, Mr. Diamond. Depression, medical conditions such as ear infections or thyroid and kidney disorders, medication side effects."

Chester piped up. "I told you that you shouldn't be mixing those old painkillers you had with that flu and cold medication or those sleeping pills."

The doctor's eyebrows lifted. "I'd like to get the name of those pain pills. I'd also like to run some other tests. But I'll need you to stay the night."

Lucas opened his mouth to argue, but Penny squeezed his shoulder. "Please, Lucas." She glanced at Chester. "For me."

Chester sniffed. "Well, I guess one night ain't gonna hurt anything." He looked at the doctor. "As long as we can stay in the same room."

"That shouldn't be a problem. But I'm afraid you'll need to get in a wheelchair to go to the room. Hospital policy." The orderly positioned the wheelchair next to the bed and started to help Chester into it, but he waved him away.

"I can get into a damned chair by myself!"

Once he was seated, the orderly pushed him toward the door and the doctor followed pushing Lucas. He paused at the doorway and turned to Cru. "I left a prescription for painkillers and some instructions on how to care for your stitches with the nurse. Be sure to get them before you leave."

Cru nodded. "Thanks, Doc."

As soon as the doctor left the room, Penny turned to him. "You're hurt?"

"It's nothing. Just a scratch."

"It's not just a scratch if you had to have stitches." There were those concerned eyes again. Drilling a hole right through him. Making him want to reach out and touch her. He didn't know how long they stood there looking at each other before Penny finally pulled her gaze away and glanced at her sister.

Evie was looking between them with a confused look. Penny might not have mentioned the kisses, but it looked like Evie had just put two and two together. Her eyes narrowed on Cru. He didn't need the warning. It might've taken him a while, but he got it now. And as much as he wanted to argue that whatever had happened between him and Evie was fifteen years ago when they were just kids, he had dated enough women to realize it wouldn't make a difference. You couldn't share your kisses between sisters. It just didn't work.

"It's late, Evie," Penny said, pulling her sister's attention away from Cru. "You should get Clint from the waiting room and take him back to the ranch." Who was Clint? Since he hadn't been able to come back to the emergency room, he was probably Evie's kid.

Evie glanced at Cru before giving her sister a hard look. "You won't be long, will you?"

"No. I just want to make sure Chester and Lucas get to their room okay."

While the Gardener sisters headed to the waiting room, Cru stopped by the nurses' station to get the prescription and instructions. By the time he got to the waiting room, Evie and whoever Clint was were gone and Penny was waiting at the elevators. The doors pinged open and she stepped in. He thought she might ignore him, but she held open the door.

"Chester and Lucas are on the second floor."

He hurried and got in the elevator. Once the doors were closed, an awkward silence reigned. He figured it was best to get things out in the open.

"Look, Penny, I'm sorry. I'm an idiot."

She turned to him and her eyebrows lifted. "And you're just figuring that out?"

He laughed. "You won't give me an inch, will you?"

"That's your problem. Too many women have given you an inch."

He couldn't argue the point. Which is probably why Penny intrigued him so much. "Fair enough. Anyway, I should've thought about the whole sister thing. I guess I just figured that it happened so long ago—I mean we were just kids having a little fun. It wasn't like we were . . ." He let the sentence drift off as he searched for the right word. Penny supplied it.

"Lovers?" She stared at him with eyes that held anger and something he couldn't quite read.

He held up his hands. "Okay, I get it. It doesn't matter what we were. All that matters is I went after her first. So I'll keep my distance."

He expected her to show some sign of regret or disappointment. She didn't. All she did was nod. The elevator doors opened on the second floor and she stepped out. Instead of following her, he remained in the elevator with his hand holding the door.

She glanced back. "Aren't you coming?"

He shook his head. "You'll do a better job then I can of making sure Chester and Lucas get settled. I think I'll head on over to the hotel."

She looked down at her scuffed boots. "Then I guess I'll be seeing you around."

He didn't know why this felt like goodbye. She was right. They would be seeing each other around. Simple was too small a town not to run into each other occasionally. But there would be no more kisses. No more starting something they couldn't stop. And maybe that was why neither one of them seemed in a hurry to leave. He just stood there holding the door and she just stood there staring at her boots until a nurse walked up.

"Are you going down?"

"Yes." Cru said and held the door as she stepped in.

The last things Cru saw before the doors closed were Penny's sad eyes.

# Chapter Eight

"HAVE YOU LOST YOUR MIND, Penelope Anne Gardener?" Her father glared across the table at her. "There is no way I'm going to let those two old horse thieves stay in my house."

"But they have nowhere else to go after they get out of the hospital, Daddy," Penny said. "They have no family and their house is burned to the ground."

"They can go to Dixon's Boardinghouse in town."

Penny stared him. "You don't mean that. You wouldn't send our neighbors to a hotel when we have plenty of room here."

Her father took a sip of his coffee. "I would two ornery old men who refuse to sell their land to me even when they're no longer herding cattle."

"You don't need any more land, Daddy."

"A rancher can always use land, but I'm more interested in their water rights."

"That's pure selfish nonsense, Hank Gardener." Sadie sailed into the dining room. The housekeeper wore her favorite lavender floral apron over a pink t-shirt and wrangler jeans. Her long steel-gray hair was pulled back in a barrette and her cheeks were flushed from cooking over a hot stove. She usually carried a tray filled with their breakfast: glasses of orange juice, bowls of oatmeal, and a plate of fresh fruit. But today, she carried a plate stacked high with iced cinnamon rolls.

Penny was surprised. Sadie hadn't made cinnamon rolls for breakfast in years. Ever since she'd overheard Doctor Simpson getting after Daddy for his high cholesterol.

Sadie gave Penny's father a stern look. "You are not going to send two old men who recently lost their home to Dixon's Boardinghouse. Reba would do her best to take care of them, but she's much too busy to keep a close eye. Here, there are plenty of people to watch out for them." She smiled at Penny and held out the plate. "Have a cinnamon roll, honey. I baked them fresh this morning with plenty of brown sugar, butter, and pecans, then doused them in cream cheese frosting."

Penny didn't know what Sadie was up to, but she followed her lead and took a gooey roll off the top. "Mmm, they look delicious. Thank you."

"You're more than welcome." Sadie turned to head back into the kitchen, but Penny's father stopped her.

"Wait just one doggone minute, Sadie Truly," he said. "You can't just waltz in here with my favorite cinnamon rolls and not offer me one."

Sadie turned and shot him a scathing look. "I

won't offer a cinnamon roll to a stubborn man who doesn't know how to be neighborly."

His eyes widened. "You're bribing me with food to let those two ornery old men stay?"

"That's exactly what I'm doing. And if you don't let Chester and Lucas stay here, you'll be cooking for yourself."

Penny stifled her giggle behind a big bite of cinnamon roll, but her father still heard and glared at her. "You think this is funny, do you?"

"No, sir," she said around her bite of gooey icing and fluffy bread.

"Well, I do." Evie walked into the dining room in a pair of Penny's pajamas. The sight of her sister here at the ranch where she belonged made Penny feel all warm and fuzzy inside—like all the pieces in the puzzle were fitting perfectly together.

"Good morning, Sadie." Evie gave Sadie a kiss on the cheek. "How did your first day as the president of the ladies' gardening club go?"

Penny had been so busy feeling guilty about kissing Cru and then worrying about the Double Diamond fire that she'd forgotten all about Sadie's big day yesterday. Leave it to Evie to remember. She always remembered every important holiday and occasion. Especially family's. And Sadie was family. After Daddy had hired her, she had become a second mother to the Gardener sisters. Since Evie loved cooking and baking, she and Sadie were especially close. And Penny often wondered if she had confided in Sadie about Clint's father.

Sadie offered the plate of cinnamon rolls to Evie.

"I must admit that I was a little nervous. Esther Tatum's shoes are going to be hard to fill, but I think I did okay."

"I'm sure you did more than okay," Evie said. "You're going to make a great president. Look how you keep up the ranch garden." She helped herself to a cinnamon roll and took a big bite, closing her eyes in ecstasy. "Mmm, these are worth their weight in gold." She glanced at Daddy and lifted an eyebrow. "Or letting Chester and Lucas stay here for a few days."

Daddy's eyebrow arched exactly like Evie's. "It will take more than a few days to repair all the damage done to their house. And I will not be bribed in my own home, Evelyn Francine." He waved a hand at Sadie. "Keep your cinnamon rolls, you ornery woman. I'm just fine with coffee."

"Stubborn mule," Sadie grumbled before she left the room.

Evie took the chair next to Penny. "She's right, Daddy. You're still as stubborn as ever."

He sent Evie a stern look. "And you're still as disrespectful as ever."

"Didn't you always teach us that respect must be earned?" Evie took another bite of her cinnamon roll as Penny cringed. Why did her sister always have to prod the bull? She quickly jumped into the conversation before it turned into an out-and-out argument.

"Aren't you glad that Evie is here, Daddy? It's been a while since we all sat down to breakfast together. I think the last time was at Christmas."

He picked up the newspaper sitting next to his plate, snapped it open, and hid behind it. "That's your sister's fault, not mine."

Evie glanced over at her and rolled her eyes.

"Don't roll your eyes at me, Evelyn Francine."

Evie glanced back at their father in surprise before she burst out laughing. Penny couldn't help but join in. Their daddy stayed hidden behind the newspaper, but Penny couldn't help noticing the suspicious rattling of the paper. Of course, when their father finally lowered it, his face was as stern as ever.

"Where's Clint?"

"He's sleeping in the guestroom." Evie licked a smudge of frosting from her finger. "I thought I'd let him sleep a few minutes more before I wake him up to head back to Abilene."

He lowered the paper. "You aren't staying?"

"Are you forgetting that I have a job, Daddy? And Clint shouldn't miss any more school than he has to."

Penny wanted to argue that one missed day of school and work wouldn't hurt. And seeing how it was Friday, they could stay the weekend. But then she remembered Clint had detention on Saturday morning so they'd have to head back soon anyway. She couldn't help feeling disappointed their visit would be so short. Her father must've felt the same way. But as always, he showed his disappointment by using hateful words.

"That boy has become too citified. He shouldn't be sleeping half the morning away like some bum."

"He's not a bum," Evie snapped. "He's a teenage kid. All teenagers like to sleep in."

"Not if they have parents who teach them good values—like getting up early and getting their chores done."

Evie threw down her napkin. "Are you calling me a bad parent, Daddy? Or are you just trying to justify working your daughters like mules when we were teenagers?"

His face turned red. "I never worked you like mules. I gave you jobs to teach you the value of hard work. Penny learned the lesson while you did everything you could to avoid it. Including running off with some boy and getting in trouble."

Penny placed a hand on Evie's arm to keep her from jumping up and leaving. "That's not true, Daddy. Evie worked just as hard as I did growing up. And even harder after she left. She put herself through college while being a single mother. Did you know she got a promotion at work? She's now in charge of loans at the bank."

He looked at Evie while Penny prayed. *Just say you're proud of her, Daddy. Please just say you're proud of her.* But before he could say anything, Clint walked in looking all sleep rumpled.

"Good morning, Grandpa."

Daddy looked at Clint and his eyes softened like they never softened with Penny and Evie. At least not after his beloved wife had passed away. It was like the burden of taking care of his daughters had taken away his softer side. But he had no trouble showing it to his grandson. "Good morning yourself. Did you sleep well?"

"Yes, sir." Clint took a chair next to his grand-father, completely unaware of the tension in the room. "Is that a cinnamon roll, Mom? Are there more?"

Evie handed him her plate. "I'm sure Sadie will bring you one, but you can have mine for now." She glared at Daddy. "I've lost my appetite."

Clint devoured the rest of the cinnamon roll in two bites and started talking. "Guess what, Grandpa. Chester and Lucas Diamond's house blew up. When they stopped in the waiting room on their way to their room, they told me the entire story. There was this huge explosion that blew glass and splintered wood everywhere. A piece of that glass stuck right in Cru's shoulder like a knife and he had to get fourteen stitches."

"Fourteen stitches? But he said it was only a scratch." The words popped out of Penny's mouth before she could stop them. Everyone in the room turned to her, but Evie stared much more intently than Clint or Daddy. She had noticed Penny and Cru's interaction at the hospital and had questioned Penny about it when they had been getting ready for bed the night before. Penny had lied and said nothing was going on between them, but Evie knew her well enough to issue a warning.

"Stay away from him, Pen. The Double Diamond boys will break your heart."

It was something Evie had learned well, and a warning Penny needed to remember. And yet, she couldn't help wondering where he had spent the night and if he'd followed the doctor's orders of how to care for his stitches.

"Who's Cru?" Daddy asked.

"Chester said he's one of the—"

"Ranch hand," Penny and Evie said at exactly the same time.

"A ranch hand?" Daddy looked at her suspiciously. "When did Chester and Lucas hire a ranch hand?"

Penny sent him an innocent look. "How would I know? I don't have time to hang out with Chester and Lucas."

"And yet you want to invite them to stay in my house."

"You are, Aunt Pen?" Clint said. "That's awesome. Then anytime you want you can listen to their cowboying stories." He looked at Daddy. "They're true cowboys."

Daddy choked on his sip of coffee. "What do you think I am?"

Clint looked confused. "I thought you were a rancher."

"Ranchers are cowboys, son." Daddy glanced over at Evie. "And if your mother would let you spend more time on the ranch, you'd know that. She should let you come here this summer and learn some good old-fashion country values."

"That would be so epic!" Clint looked at his mother. "What about it, Mom? Could I come and spend the summer with Grandpa and Aunt Pen?"

Evie sent Daddy an exasperated look. "I don't think that's a good idea."

"Why not?" Clint asked. "You said yourself that you were worried about me staying at home this summer—worried that I'd get in trouble with Tommy. If I'm here, there will be no way I can hang out with Tommy."

"Who's Tommy?" Daddy asked.

"Just Clint's friend," Penny said before she turned to Evie. "It isn't such a bad idea. We could use the extra hand and you wouldn't have to worry about Clint while you're at work. It would be like sending him to camp except with family." And if Clint fell in love with the ranch, it would be that much easier to convince Evie to come home.

"Come on, Mom. Ple-e-ease." Clint glanced at Daddy. "Help me out, Grandpa. Talk her into letting me come."

Hank Gardener never begged, or even asked for that matter, but he did bargain. After only a few minutes thought, he spoke. "I'll make you a deal, Evelyn Francine. If you let Clint come for the summer, I'll let Chester and Lucas stay here for as long as they want. Not in the house, mind you, but in the bunkhouse. I might even send a few boys over to help them clean up after the fire."

The offer of help didn't surprise Penny. Her daddy had a soft side. He just rarely showed it.

Evie lifted her eyebrow. "Are you bribing me, Daddy? I thought Hank Gardener didn't deal with bribes."

"I don't take them, but I'm not above offering them if it gets me what I want."

It was as close as their father was going to get

to saying he would love to spend time with his grandson, and Penny hoped Evie would recognize that and give just a little.

Evie glanced at Clint. "Are you sure you want to spend the entire summer with your grumpy grandpa?"

"And your sweet aunt," Penny piped up.

Clint laughed. "Hell yeah, I do."

Daddy laughed before sending him a stern look. "Watch your mouth in front of ladies, Clint."

"Yes, sir. Sorry, Aunt Pen. Sorry, Mom." Clint sent his mom another beseeching look and she finally gave in.

"Fine." She held up a finger. "But only one month."

Clint held up two. Penny mimicked him. And Daddy followed suit.

Evie shook her head. "Obviously, I'm outnumbered. Okay, two months. But that's all."

Clint let out a whoop and held up a hand to high-five Daddy. Penny was surprised when her father complied. Evie rolled her eyes at Penny as Sadie walked back into the dining room carrying a large tray of food.

"Now that that's settled. Let's have breakfast." She set down the tray and picked up the plate of cinnamon rolls, offering one to Daddy. "See what a little compromise will get you, Hank Gardener?"

# CHAPTER NINE

CRU WAS DREAMING. HE KNEW he was dreaming, but he didn't want to wake up. Not when he was lying in a field of bluebonnets with Penny. It wasn't a sexual dream. They weren't naked or getting hot and heavy. They were fully clothed and lying on their sides looking at each other. But what he loved about the dream was that her expression wasn't guarded. Everything she felt was written on her face and in her clear blue eyes. She was happy. And her happiness made him happy. Her soft smile made him feel like he could jump the moon.

She reached out and cradled his jaw in her cool hand. "I'm here. I'm staying right here forever." She leaned in and . . . licked his face.

He blinked awake and stared in confusion at the roof of the barn before a horse's head blocked his view and a long tongue gave him another wet kiss from chin to forehead. He pushed Misty away and sat up, wiping off the horse slobber.

"Thanks for the good morning kiss, girl, but I

prefer my women to use less tongue."

Misty shook her head as if to say she didn't believe him.

He laughed. "Fine. I don't mind a little tongue, but from two-legged women." He yawned and started to stretch, but stopped when pain shot through his shoulder. The pain reminded him of the fire and caused his good humor to fade.

He had come back to the ranch the night before to see if he could savage anything from the fire, but all he'd found was a pile of ashes. Except for Chester's old truck and the barn, Chester and Lucas had lost everything. Too depressed and tired to head back into town, Cru had taken a pain-killer and bedded down in the barn with Misty. It was no wonder he'd dreamed of Penny. His last thought before he fell asleep was of her sad eyes right before the elevator closed. He knew she felt the attraction between them too. But it was too late. He'd already screwed things up. Looking back, he realized he and Evie hadn't even had anything in common. He'd just been a horny teenager. But since there was no going back, he needed to accept the situation and move on.

He got to his feet and tried to work out the stiff-ness in his shoulder. The open barn door caught his attention and he moved out of the stall and stood in the doorway. He hoped things would look better in the light of day, but the charred ruins of the house looked even worse in the bright morning sun. He pulled his cellphone out of his jeans pocket and dialed Logan's number.

"Hey, Cru." Logan's breath huffed through the receiver.

"Did I catch you at a bad time?"

"No. I'm just at the gym working out on the treadmill." So that was the steady thump Cru could hear in the background. "How are things going? Last time we talked, it sounded like Lucas and Chester were doing better."

Cru rubbed the sleep from his eyes with his thumb and forefinger. "Yeah, well, they're not doing quite as well now." He paused before dropping the bomb. "Lucas blew up the kitchen."

The thumping stopped. "He what?"

"He left the gas range on and the firemen think the water heater pilot clicked on and ignited it."

"Are they okay? Are you okay?"

"We're all fine. But it's a miracle." Cru relayed the entire story. When he was finished, it took Logan a moment to answer.

"Well, hell. Where are Chester and Lucas now?"

"I talked them into staying at the hospital for the night. Or not me as much as Penny and Evie Gardener. Those two girls can talk them into just about anything."

"Evie's back?"

Cru walked to the stall and sat down on a bale of hay to pull on his socks and boots. "Not for good. She came to make sure Chester and Lucas were okay."

Logan snorted. "Or more likely she and her sister saw a chance to get the Double Diamond Ranch for their daddy. Hank Gardener has always wanted to get his hands on the land."

"And Chester and Lucas should sell it to them. It would solve a lot of problems."

"They can find other buyers if they decide to sell. Hank is an asshole."

Cru laughed. "Don't tell me you're still holding a grudge against Hank for throwing us off his property when he caught us swimming at Mesquite Springs."

"Among other things," Logan said dryly. The thumping started back up. "So what are Chester and Lucas going to do? They have to be devastated about losing their house."

Cru pulled on his boots, wincing when pain shot through his shoulder. "They're pretty upset, and I can't blame them. They lost everything. And the even sadder part is they let their insurance lapse so there's no money to rebuild. But maybe that's for the best. Maybe this will make it easier to talk them into selling the ranch and moving somewhere else. Somewhere someone can keep an eye on them."

"You're right, but I just can't see those two cowboys in some retirement home. They'll absolutely hate it."

"What other choices do we have? I no longer have a home. You want them to come live with you?"

"Chester and Lucas would hate my condo as much as a retirement home. The only place they'll be happy is on the Double Diamond Ranch." He huffed in and out for a moment before he spoke. "What if we could rebuild the ranch house and make it a little more senior friendly?"

"Do you have money for that? Because I don't."

"Most of my money is tied up in my business, but I'm sure I could scrape together a little. It won't be enough to build a house, but it would be a start. And maybe I could ask some of the other boys to chip in too. Val seems to be doing pretty well with his bestselling thrillers. He should be able to help out. And maybe Sawyer, Linc, and Holden could too."

"And then what?" Cru couldn't help pointing out that a new house wasn't going to fix the biggest problem. "They still need help, Logan. They might not need twenty-four-hour care now, but they will. Right now, they need someone to cook their meals and make sure they don't blow up the house. It's too bad Penny can't do it."

"I wouldn't trust a Gardener as far as I could throw one."

"We could trust Penny. She's a good woman."

Logan laughed. "A good woman? What happened to her being hot?"

"She's still hot, but she's also a good woman."

The thumping stopped. "Okay, what's going on between you and Penny? I've never heard you refer to a girl you find attractive as a good woman. You comment about their body or how great they are in bed, but you never comment about their character. You like her?"

"So what if I do? I happen to like a lot of women."

"In a sexual way. You've never liked a woman for her character."

Logan had a point. Penny *was* different. Cru didn't just like her looks. He liked what was underneath all that gorgeous red hair, azure blue eyes, and cute freckles. He liked her feistiness and the way she handled a horse. He liked that she didn't act like a spoiled, rich rancher's daughter when she talked to people in town and how she seemed to really care about them. He liked the kindness she'd shown Chester and Lucas. The love she had for the land and her ranch. And her loyalty to her family—even if it kept her out of his arms. Although maybe he didn't like that as much as he respected it.

"Penny is different from the other women I've known," he said as he got to his feet. "Which is why I would totally trust her to take good care of Lucas and Chester. But she doesn't have the time. She has a full time job working on the Gardener Ranch."

The thumping returned. "Well, I'm sure we could find someone in town who would be willing to do it if they got paid. I can probably get enough together to rebuild the house, but not to pay for help. Like it or not, Chester and Lucas might have to sell some of their beloved land."

"Now all we have to do is convince them of that. In fact, why don't you give them a call? They might listen to you. Chester always had a soft spot for you."

"That was before I ruined his and Lucas's plans to run the boy's ranch."

"You ruined? What do you mean?"

There was a long stretch of silence punctuated only by the thumping of feet on a treadmill. Finally, Logan spoke. "After we left that summer, I got a wild hair to go back. So I stole a car . . . I ran into Hank Gardener and we got into it. He called the sheriff and I had to spend a year in a juvenile detention center. I'm sure he also riled up the townsfolk and got them to sign the petition to close the Double Diamond boy's ranch."

Cru was stunned. "So that's why you hate him. Why didn't you ever tell me?"

"Because there's no use talking about the past. You can't change it." The thumping stopped. "Listen, I need to get to work."

"Oh no. You're not going to drop a bomb like that and not give me all the details. Whose car did you steal and how did you run into Hank if you were going to see Chester and Lucas? And how exactly did you get into it? Are we talking words or fists?"

"You know I've never been as good with words as I am with fists. Now I really need to go. I'll call you after I talk with the other guys. Do you need money before then? I didn't think about new clothes and hotel accommodations."

They would definitely need a place to stay and new clothes. All Cru had were the clothes on his back, and the shirt wasn't even his. The triage nurse had given him a green surgical scrub shirt to wear since his t-shirt had been ripped and covered in blood. But he refused to ask for money from Logan. He felt bad enough that he couldn't chip in on a new house for Chester and Lucas. But he did have enough in his travel fund to cover new clothes and a hotel. Although if they had to stay in a hotel for longer then a month, he'd be screwed.

"I got it covered, but thanks, man."

"You're the one who should be thanked. I appreciate you being there, Cru. And I know Lucas and Chester appreciate it too. I'll talk to you soon."

After he hung up, Cru stood there for a second before he shook his head. He knew Logan had a bad temper, but getting into a fistfight with Hank Gardener? No wonder the town had wanted to stop Chester and Lucas from bringing in any more delinquent boys to their ranch.

A nudge from Misty reminded him that the horse needed to be fed. Once he'd fed her, he released her into the corral. Since the corral was made up of only a few posts and some broken down railing, the horse could've easily escaped. But for some reason, the old mare didn't seem to realize that. Or maybe, like Chester and Lucas, she just didn't want to leave her home.

After Cru filled up her water trough, he drank from the hose and splashed the sleep from his face. He had more than a day's growth of beard and wished he could shave, but his razor was somewhere beneath a pile of charred wood.

Thinking about what else might be beneath the fire damage, he grabbed a shovel and started searching through the rubble. He found Chester's shotgun, some of Lucas's cast iron pots—including his old Dutch oven—some of their rodeo belt buckles, and a large metal lockbox. They were all covered in soot and he carried them into the barn to clean them up. As he wiped off the lockbox, he noticed that the back hinges had melted through. Curious as to what Chester and Lucas would find important, he opened the lid. He hoped he'd find gold or stacks of money inside. Instead, he found pictures of him and the other boys who had attended the ranch that summer. They were a motley-looking crew. He looked like an arrogant punk. Which was exactly what he'd been.

His picture was stapled to a questionnaire with a short bio. He recognized Father Stephen's neat, precise handwriting immediately. Cru's chest tightened. He tried to ignore the pain, but his chest tightened even more when he read what Father Stephen had written.

*Cru Cassidy was deserted by his mother in a bus station bathroom when he was four years old. Upon his arrival at St. James's, he was convinced his mother would return for him. When she didn't, he grew angry and hard to handle—throwing uncontrollable temper tantrums that made it difficult to place him with a family. He's outgrown that anger, and now hides his pain beneath a charming smile. He needs lots of understanding and encouragement.*

He dropped the papers as if they had caught on fire as memories of that scared, angry boy welled up from the dark place he'd tried to hide them. Once again, he was standing at the front window of the orphanage watching and waiting for a mother who never showed up and wondering what he had done to make her leave.

The avalanche of emotions he'd tried so hard to hold back sucker punched him hard in the chest, knocking all the air out of his lungs. And try as he might he couldn't pull it back in.

Struggling for breath, he stumbled out into the sunlight. He took big gulps of air, trying to fill his lungs. But the extra oxygen didn't make him feel better. It only made him feel worse. He grew light-headed and dizzy. The world around him started to spin, and before he knew it he was on the ground with his cheek pressed against the hard earth.

The last thought he had before he lost consciousness was that he didn't want to die alone.

# CHAPTER TEN

PENNY FELT HAPPIER THAN SHE'D felt in a long time as she rode toward the Double Diamond Ranch. Not only had Evie and their father kept from fighting for the remainder of breakfast, but Evie had also agreed to let Clint stay the summer at the ranch. And if Penny could get Clint to love the ranch and want to move back, she was sure she could get her sister to agree. Of course, she still had to deal with the entire marriage thing. But Evie hadn't said 'yes' yet. And Penny could only hope it was because, deep down, she knew she couldn't marry someone she didn't love.

It looked like Evie didn't love Cru anymore either. At the hospital, they hadn't shown any signs of still having feelings for each other. And Penny had been watching closely. The only one who had reacted like a love struck idiot was Penny. But she hadn't been able to hide her concern when she heard Cru had needed stitches. Nor could she keep from feeling miserable when she and Cru had said goodbye.

She knew staying away from each other was for the best. But even now the thought of never being able to taste Cru's lips again diminished her bubble of happiness. It completely burst when she rounded the copse of trees and saw the blackened remains of Chester and Lucas's house.

Suddenly, she realized just how lucky Cru, Chester, and Lucas were to be alive. She also realized how much Chester and Lucas had lost to the fire. Not only the house, but also their furniture, their clothes, their memories. They didn't just need a place to stay. They needed help restoring their lives. She intended to make sure they got that help. Maybe she could talk to the pastors of the two churches in town and see if they could take up a collection. But first, she had to convince them to come stay with her and her father. Since they didn't like Hank, it wouldn't be easy. But she refused to let them go to a hotel room, or even worse, sleep in the barn.

And speaking of the barn…

Penny reined in Severus when she saw the bright red Porsche parked in front. Her heart did a little leap in her chest. What was he doing there? She thought he was staying at the boardinghouse in town. He had probably come by to check on Misty. Which was exactly why Penny was there. She'd planned to bring the horse back to the Gardener stables. If Cru was caring for the horse, it was best if she turned around and headed home. But before she could, something on the ground by the barn caught her attention. She looked closer and realized it wasn't something but someone. Her heart lodged in her throat as she urged Severus into a gallop. When she reached Cru, she reined in and swung down from the saddle.

"Cru!" When he didn't respond, she knelt down next to him and pulled her phone from her pocket. She tried to dial 911, but her hands were shaking so badly she kept pressing the wrong numbers.

"Shit!" As she tried again, Cru rolled to his back and blinked at her.

"I've never heard you cuss before."

She lowered her phone. "Oh my God." She wilted over his body in relief, her head pressing against the strong, steady beat of his heart. "I thought you were dead."

He took a deep breath, lifting her head. "So did I."

She started to rise, but his arms came around her and held tight. There was something desperate in his hug. Something that tore at her soul. She relaxed back against him.

"What happened?" she asked.

He took another deep breath. "I don't know. I just passed out. I guess those painkillers the doc gave me for my shoulder were stronger than I thought. Or maybe it was just from lack of food."

She lifted her head. "You haven't eaten?"

"I just woke up and was headed into town to get something to eat when it happened."

"You slept here? I thought you were going to the boardinghouse in Simple after you left the hospital."

"I wanted to see if I could salvage anything from the fire and was too tired to drive back into town." His gaze lowered to her mouth, and she suddenly realized how close they were. Close enough that she could feel his warm breath against her face when he spoke. "What did you have for breakfast?"

She blinked. "Excuse me?"

"You've got something right there." He brushed a finger over the corner of her mouth and a shiver of heat raced through her. It settled in her panties when he stuck his finger in his mouth and gently sucked. "Frosting? You had cake for breakfast?"

"Cinnamon rolls," she said breathlessly. She knew she was still looking at his mouth, but she couldn't seem to stop herself. Especially when he licked his bottom lip.

"Damn, that sounds good. I'm starving."

She was starving too. Starving for the one decadent slice of dessert that she couldn't have. She pushed against his chest until he released her, and then quickly got to her feet. "Then we better get you something to eat." She slipped her cellphone in her back pocket and held out a hand.

"We?" He got to his feet without her help.

"You can't drive. Not when you're on strong painkillers." Without a thought, she brushed the dirt off his jaw. The stubbles of his morning beard were prickly and sent tingles down her arm. She jerked her hand back and stuffed it in her back pocket so it wouldn't be tempted to touch him again.

He studied her for a moment before he smiled.

"Are you always such a mother hen?"

"I'm not a mother hen."

"I don't know what else you'd call it. You mother Chester and Lucas. And now you're trying to mother me."

"Maybe I'm just trying to keep you from killing yourself . . . or someone else. I've seen the way you drive when you're sober. Strung out on pain pills, you'll be a danger to everyone on the road." She held out a hand. "Now give me your keys."

"I'm not strung out on pain pills. I took one last night. Besides, I promised Lucas and Chester I'd be back to get them before noon. I'll grab a donut on the way."

"Sugar is the last thing you need. You need a full breakfast with plenty of protein. You also need something bigger than that two-seater rocket of yours if you plan to pick up Chester and Lucas."

"I was going to take Chester's truck."

"Fine, but I'm driving. Now give me the keys."

He scowled as he stuck his hand in his front pocket and pulled out a set of keys. "Do you even know how to drive a shift stick?"

"My granddaddy taught me how to drive his old Chevy truck so I think I can manage." She took the keys from him and put them in her front pocket. "Let me just take care of Misty and put Severus in the barn, then we can go."

"I took care of Misty." He glanced around. "And your demon horse seems to be missing."

Placing two fingers in her mouth, Penny whistled loudly. Severus came trotting around the barn.

Cru shook his head. "I guess all males do your bidding."

"Only well-behaved ones." She took Severus's bridle and led him into the barn.

On the way to the stall, she noticed a piece of paper on the ground and leaned down to pick it up so Severus wouldn't trample it. When she saw Cru's picture attached, she stopped short and read through the questionnaire. When she finished, she felt like Severus had trampled her heart.

Cru was an orphan? He'd been so cocky and sure of himself. She'd always figured he was just a wild teenager whose parents hadn't been able to handle him. But he hadn't had parents. Not even foster parents. Penny had been eleven when her mother passed away and it had seemed like the end of the world. How much harder would it have been for a four-year-old to lose his mother?

Especially when she was all he had.

"Penny?" Cru's voice caused her to jump guiltily and glance over her shoulder. He stood in the doorway with the sunlight outlining his tall, lean body. As a teenager, she'd seen him as a charming bad boy. After he got Evie pregnant, she'd seen him as an irresponsible jerk. In the last few weeks, she'd seen him as Lucas and Chester's caregiver—a man she couldn't exactly admire, but couldn't hate either. And now, she couldn't help seeing him as a little four-year-old boy frantically searching for his mother.

"Do you need some help?" he asked.

She turned back around so he wouldn't see her

tears and quickly folded the paper and stuffed it into her front pocket. "I'm fine. I was just texting my dad to let him know I wouldn't be at the branding pen until later today."

"You can get back to work. I'm really okay."

Cru might be okay, but she wasn't. Cru was no longer the bad boy. He was a lost boy. And Penny knew what it was like to be lost after losing a parent.

"No," she said. "I'll drive you. Daddy can survive without me for a little while." She took her time removing Severus's saddle and bridle, hoping to get her emotions in check. But they unraveled again when she walked out to see Cru leaning against Chester's truck. He had put on his cowboy hat and a pair of aviator sunglasses. With the dark shadow of his day's growth of beard, he looked even more of a sexy bad boy than usual. But now she knew the reason behind his bad boy ways.

Her eyes welled with tears, and she quickly tried to brush them away. But he saw and straightened from the truck.

"Are you okay?"

"I'm fine," she lied. "I just have hay fever."

He smiled. "A cowgirl with an allergy to hay. Now that's funny." He opened the truck door for her. "Come on, cowgirl, this cowboy needs to eat."

On the drive in to Simple, Cru told her about the items he'd salvaged from Chester and Lucas's house. But she had trouble concentrating on the conversation while her mind was still stuck on the image of a little boy standing alone in a bus station.

Cru handed her a faded bandanna. "Your eyes are watering again. You really need to think about getting some allergy medicine."

"Thank you." She took the bandanna and blotted her eyes before handing it back. "It sounds like Chester and Lucas will have to replace almost everything. I'm going to talk to the pastors of the churches in town and see if they won't take up a collection. It probably won't be enough to cover a new house, but it might be enough to buy the materials and I know we could get some volunteers to help rebuild. Maybe we could even have a house raising."

"You mean like a barn raising? That's a good idea. Logan wants to chip in and he's going to see if some of the other boys can too. You remember Logan, don't you?"

"Of course I remember him. The tall, dark, and brooding boy. Evie thought he was stuck-up, but I liked Logan. He was always nice to me."

"Because you were a cute kid who told funny knock-knock jokes."

"They weren't funny. They were stupid."

"I didn't think so."

She glanced over at him and saw that he was studying her. She got lost in the green pastures of his eyes for only a few seconds before she returned her attention to the road. "Then we have a plan for rebuilding their house. Now all I need to do is talk them into staying at the Gardener Ranch."

"You're going to invite them to stay at your ranch?"

"It only makes sense—we're their closest neighbors. They can't afford to stay at Dixon's Boardinghouse indefinitely, and we have plenty of room."

"That's real nice of you, Penny. But I was planning on paying for their hotel rooms. And they don't exactly get along with your daddy."

"Well, it's time they got over it. They've been feuding with each other for decades and it's sheer stubbornness. Maybe this is the perfect way to end that feud."

Cru snorted. "Good luck. I can't see those stubborn fools giving in on anything. I'm not even sure they'll be okay with people raising money to rebuild their house. They hate charity. And if they view raising money to build a new house as charity, they'll view your offer of a place to stay the same way."

He had a good point. Penny puzzled the problem over as they headed down the dirt road. When they passed a herd of Gardener cattle, an idea hit her. "What about if I turn it around? And instead of making it out like I'm helping them, I'll make it out like they would be helping me?"

"How are you going to do that?"

"I'm going to offer them jobs."

"Jobs? Please don't tell me you're going to let Lucas become your new cook."

She laughed. "I doubt Sadie would give up her position. But I'm sure we can find some other things for them to do around the ranch."

"I don't know. It doesn't sound too safe to have

a couple of old guys wandering around a working ranch."

"Then you'll just have to come along to keep an eye on them."

Once the words were out, Penny felt more than a little stunned. What was she doing? She had thought it was hard resisting him before. How much harder would it be if she saw him every day? Not to mention how pissed Evie would be once she found out. But not even her sister's anger could change Penny's mind. She couldn't stand the thought of him being at Dixon's Boardinghouse all alone. When her mother died, she'd had her sister and father to help her get through the loss. Cru had no family after his mother left him.

At least, no family he knew about.

Penny had always gone along with Evie's decision not to tell Cru about his son. But now that she knew about Cru's mother, she felt a heavy guilt for keeping his son from him. He might be a playboy who had no desire to settle down, but maybe having a son would change that. It wasn't her secret to tell, but she could try to convince Evie to do it.

"You want me to move to the Gardener Ranch?" he asked. She glanced over to see him looking at her with bewilderment. "I'm sorry, but I'm a little confused. I thought I was off-limits because of the entire sister thing."

She turned onto the highway. "You are."

"And yet you're inviting me to stay at your ranch where we'll see each other every day."

"Are you saying you can't resist me, Cru Cassidy?" She kept her eyes on the highway, but she could feel the heat of his gaze sliding over her. Her heart picked up speed and sweat collected between her palms and the steering wheel.

"I can resist," he said in a low, sexy voice. "The question is . . . can you?"

His cockiness had her lifting her chin. "I think I can manage. You aren't that irresistible. Just annoying. And to help out Chester and Lucas, I'm willing to put up with an annoying Double Diamond bad boy for a few weeks."

Cru laughed. "Fine, Miss Penny Gardener, you've struck a deal. I'll come to the ranch and help you keep an eye on those two old cowboys. But you need to know one thing. I'm not going to hide from you. If this bad boy tempts you beyond your ability to resist that's your problem, not mine."

# CHAPTER ELEVEN

CHESTER AND LUCAS DIDN'T PUT up as much of a fight about staying at the Gardener Ranch as Cru thought they would. Of course, it wasn't easy fighting a beautiful redhead with big, innocent blue eyes. All Penny had to do was tell them how much she needed their help at the ranch and they were toast. And Cru wasn't much better. He had no business staying at the Gardener Ranch. Now that Lucas and Chester were settled into the bunkhouse with more than enough people to watch out for them, he should be cruising down the highway in his Porsche on his way to sandy beaches filled with suntanned, half-naked beauties.

Instead he was standing in a used car lot in Abilene getting ready to do something really stupid.

"It's a nice car." The salesman's words were casual, but the gleam in his eyes was rabid as he walked around the sports car. "I could maybe trade you for that king-cab Ram truck you're interested in, but you'd have to give me a couple thousand cash to go along with it. Cars like this don't sell real well in Abilene." He glanced at Cru's green scrub shirt. "You a doc?"

"Nope." Cru smiled. "A car salesman. So let's cut through the bullshit, shall we? I know exactly what this car is worth and it's worth more than any car you have on this lot. If you can't sell it here, I'm sure you'll have no trouble selling it somewhere else. So here's my deal. Not only are you going to trade me that used Dodge Ram, but you're also going to pay me cash. I'm thinking . . ." He used his finger to write a number in the dust on the hood of the Ram truck.

The gleam faded from the salesman's eyes and he shook his head. "No can do, partner. There's no way I can recoup my money if I strike that deal."

Cru shrugged. "Then I guess I'll try one of your competitors." He got back in the Porsche and started the engine, making sure to give it just enough gas to cause the engine to growl. Before he could even pop it into first gear the salesman was tapping on his window. Not an hour later, Cru was heading out of the lot in the Dodge pickup with a hefty check in his pocket.

His next stop was a western store where he bought shirts, jeans, and boot socks. Since he had done laundry for Chester and Lucas, he knew their sizes and what styles they liked. Then he headed to a Walmart where he picked up underwear and toiletries. He used his credit card for the purchases. The check for the Porsche he planned to add to Chester and Lucas's house fund. When he finished his shopping, he grabbed a Quarter Pounder, fries, and a Coke at a McDonald's before he headed back to Simple.

Once on the highway, he should've felt depressed when he stepped on the gas to pass a semitruck and only inched past it at a snail's pace. But he didn't. There was something nice about sitting in a big ol' truck with the windows down and a good country tune blaring from the speakers. As he passed, the trucker waved and he waved back—something he couldn't have done if he'd shot past like a rocket. He had to wonder if you missed a lot of things when you went too fast.

On the dirt road to the Gardener Ranch, he couldn't help opening the truck up. Trucks handled bumpy terrain much better than Porsches. He was having so much fun off-roading that he drove right past the white sedan parked by the side of the road. In the rearview mirror, he could see a woman sitting behind the wheel fanning at the dust trail he'd left behind.

He quickly stepped on the brakes and backed up until he was even with her open window. "Beg pardon, ma'am. I didn't see you sitting there."

The woman who stared back at him didn't look like she belonged on a country dirt road in the middle of nowhere. She looked like she belonged in a library behind a tall desk piled high with books. Her dark hair was pulled back in a smooth, tight bun and she wore those cute, nerdy, black-framed glasses that city girls seemed to like.

"That's understandable given the speed you were

going," she stated before she dismissed him and went back to looking at the phone she held in her hand.

"Car trouble?" he asked.

"No." She tapped at the screen of her phone. "I'm attempting to get my global positioning system to work."

It was the first time Cru had heard anyone refer to their GPS by its full name. "It's easy to lose a signal way out here. But I'd be happy to point you in the right direction." He smiled. "And don't worry, I won't send you to have sweet tea with my mama."

Her big hazel eyes glanced up at him and she blinked behind the lenses of her glasses. "Why would you send me to have sweet tea with your mother?"

"It was a joke. Obviously, a bad one. It's what happens in the country song 'Good Directions and Turnip Greens.'"

She still looked baffled. "Shouldn't it be called Good Directions and Sweet Tea? What do turnip greens have to do with the song? Does the mother serve turnip greens too? Because the leafy vegetation on the top of turnips isn't very appropriate for a tea. Usually one would serve finger sandwiches, scones, and petit fours."

He squinted at her. Nope, this woman didn't belong on a country road in rural Texas. He wasn't even sure she belonged on earth. "Well, I'll sure remember that if I ever have a tea party. So where are you headed?"

"I'm not at liberty to say."

Cru pushed his cowboy hat up on his forehead. "Well, ma'am, I hate to point this out, but if you don't tell me where you're headed, I can't help you get there. And you could be sitting here waiting for your global positioning system until the cows come home." At her confused look, he clarified. "For a very long time."

She looked at her phone, then back at him. "Very well, but I hope I can count on your discretion. I did some research and gossip is the number one pastime for small rural areas."

Now he was intrigued. Why would this woman want him to be discreet? What was she up to? "I'm not much of a gossiper."

She studied him for another moment before she finally nodded. "Very well. I'm looking for the Gardener Ranch."

"You're in luck. That's where I'm headed."

"Are you Hank Gardener? When I talked to you on the phone you sounded older."

So she had never met the Gardeners. Things just kept getting more and more interesting. "Nope. I just work at the ranch." It wasn't a lie. He intended to work for his room and board while he was there. Chester and Lucas could take charity from Penny, but he wasn't about to. He reached his hand out the window. "Cru Cassidy."

She hesitantly shook his hand. "Devlin McMillian."

"Nice to meet you, Devlin. If you follow me, I'll have you there in a jiffy . . . quickly."

On the way to the Gardener Ranch, he kept

glancing in his rearview mirror at the woman following him. Not because he was attracted to her—although even with her hair all twigged up and those huge glasses, she was a nice-looking woman—but because she'd gotten his curiosity up with her secretive behavior. The car was definitely a rental. And why would a prim and proper city girl rent a car and drive all the way out to Gardener Ranch on business?

He became even more curious when they arrived at the ranch. He had no more than hopped out of his truck to open her door when Hank Gardener came out of the house.

"Can I help you?" He directed the question at Cru.

Cru didn't know how much Penny had told her father, so he kept it simple. "Cru Cassidy. Penny hired me on. And this is Devlin McMillian. Or do you already know each other?"

Hank's gazed snapped over to Devlin, who was getting out of her car before coming back to Cru. "Stow your things in the bunkhouse and I'll be out to show you around when I'm through here."

Penny had already shown him around that morning with Chester and Lucas, but he nodded anyway. "Yes, sir." He walked to his truck slowly so he could eavesdrop.

"I wasn't expecting you, Ms. McMillian." Hank didn't sound happy. Of course, from what Cru knew of the man, he was never happy. "You were supposed to call me when you got into town so we could set up a meeting."

"I thought it would be more expedient if I came here," Devlin said. "The sooner I start surveying, the sooner—"

Hank cut her off. "We can discuss this inside, Ms. McMillian. Cru!" Cru glanced back to see Hank scowling at him. "I hope you're not as slow at working as you are at walking."

"No, sir." He pulled open his truck door and climbed in, then drove around to the bunkhouse where he'd left Chester and Lucas watching television. Before he got out of the truck, he Googled Devlin McMillian on his cellphone. Rather than search through the entries, he searched images until he found her picture with the same glasses and topknot.

It turned out she was a geoscientist. Cru had sold an electric car to a geoscientist once and the guy had told him all about his job. What business did Hank Gardener have with a scientist who studied the solid, liquid, and gaseous matter of the earth? There seemed to be only one answer. Hank had discovered oil deposits on his land. It was a little annoying that the rich got richer while people like Lucas and Chester were shit out of luck. Of course, if there turned out to be oil on Hank's land, there could be oil on the Double Diamond. And wouldn't that be a lucky break?

He pocketed his phone and hopped out, looking forward to a nice long shower. Unfortunately, when he got inside, Chester and Lucas weren't sitting in front of the television where he'd left them. They were nowhere to be found. Which meant his shower would have to wait. Thinking that the barn was the most likely place they'd be, he headed there first. He didn't find them, but he did find a three-legged dog.

"Hey, there, buddy." He squatted down to scratch the dog's ears and received a friendly lick for his troubles.

"Trixie's a female." Raul, whom Cru had met earlier, came out of one of the stalls holding a rake.

Cru continued to pet Trixie. "How did she lose her leg?"

"We don't know. Miss Penny found her hobbling along the side of the road. She was half-starved and already a tripod."

So Penny had brought the dog home. He should've known. The woman seemed to collect misfits. Cru shook his head as he stood. "Have you seen Chester and Lucas around? They're not in the bunkhouse."

"No, but that might explain why two of the horses are missing."

Cru heaved a sigh. He should've known the two old guys wouldn't stay put. "Do you mind if I take a horse and go look for them?"

"Just pick one out, and I'll saddle it up for you."

He could've chosen one of the mild-mannered mares, but instead he chose the black stallion. He'd been itching to ride Severus since he'd first seen Penny on him.

"Are you sure?" Raul asked. "This horse doesn't much care for anyone riding him but Miss Penny."

"I think I can manage." But it wasn't easy. Severus

started acting up as soon as he settled into the saddle. Cru didn't fight him. He just kept a firm seat in the saddle and let him get his fidgeting out. After a while, Severus calmed down and accepted his new rider.

"I'd check the branding pens first," Raul said. He gave Cru directions.

Cru kept Severus in a sedate trot for about half a mile before he gave the horse free rein and they took off. He would've enjoyed every second of the fast ride if he hadn't been so worried about Chester and Lucas. The thought of one old guy with a sprained ankle and the other half blind wandering around the ranch on horseback scared the crap out of him.

It turned out his fear was uncalled for. When he arrived at the branding pens, he discovered Chester and Lucas were just fine. In fact, they were more than fine. They looked like they were having the time of their lives as they herded Angus cows into the cattle chute to wait for their turn to be branded. They were whistling and flapping their coiled ropes as they maneuvered their cutting horses first one way and then the other to separate cows. At the end of the chute, Penny and a ranch hand stood at the cage used to hold each cow for branding and ear marking. She glanced up when Cru drew closer to the pens and Severus nickered a greeting, but she immediately went back to work.

Sweat dampened the back of her western shirt and glistened on her neck between the two braids that hung over her shoulders. She worked quickly and efficiently with the ranch hand and within minutes, they had a cow ear marked and branded before releasing it into the corral with the rest of the cattle.

Once she was finished, she walked over to the railing where Cru sat on Severus and pulled off her hat, wiping the sweat from her brow with her sleeve. "That's my horse."

He grinned. "Are you calling me a horse thief?"

"Nope, just a cocky cowboy who thinks he can take what he wants." She glanced back at Chester and Lucas. "I tried to send them back to the ranch, but you know how well they listen. I believe their exact words were 'You hired us to work and we're working.'" She shook her head. "Obviously, my plan backfired."

"I don't know about that. I haven't seen them so happy since I got here. Neither one of them are steady on their feet, but they sure as hell can ride. It seems age doesn't matter in the saddle."

"Once a cowboy, always a cowboy, my grandpa used to say." The ranch hand who'd been working with Penny stepped up next to her and pulled off his hat. He was younger than Cru had first thought. Young and handsome with eyes that sparkled a little too much when they landed on Penny. "I've got the next cow ready, Miss Penny."

"Thanks, Dylan. This is Cru Cassidy. He's here to help me keep an eye on Chester and Lucas. This is Dylan Matheson. He just hired on, but he's become my right hand man." Penny playfully tapped the brim of Dylan's hat and an emotion settled in the pit of Cru's stomach. An emotion he hadn't felt before and couldn't quite place…until they went back to the cattle crush and Cru noticed how well they worked together. They didn't need to say a word to each other as they went about their job. When Penny had trouble sliding the head bar into place, Dylan was right there to help her out, placing his hand next to hers to give her his added strength.

That's when Cru identified the emotion.

Jealousy. Hard, unrelenting jealousy that slammed into his body and had him swinging down from Severus and securing the horse's reins before climbing over the pen's railing.

"Why don't you take a break, Dylan," Cru said in a voice that didn't sound at all like the easy-going person he strived to be. "I'll help Penny."

Both Dylan and Penny glanced back at him with confusion. And they had every right to be confused. Hell, he was completely baffled by the emotions that swirled around inside him. But that didn't stop him from moving next to Penny as if he were staking his claim.

Her eyes squinted at him from beneath the brim of her hat. "I don't think that's a good idea. I don't want you pulling out your stitches. And do you even know how to brand cattle?"

"My shoulder is fine, and I did my fair share of branding on the Double Diamond. Back then, we had to rope each cow and use a branding iron straight from the fire. This looks a lot easier."

"It is if you know what you're doing," Dylan said.

Cru mad-dogged him. "I think I can figure it out."

Dylan stared back at him before he glanced at Penny. "You want him to take over, Miss Penny?"

"It's fine, Dylan. You go check on Billy and Sam and make sure they're bringing in those cows from the east pasture like I told them and not taking a nap under some tree."

Dylan shot Cru one more hard look before he nodded and walked toward a horse that was tied up at the railing.

When he was gone, Penny looked at Cru. "You want to play cowboy, you're going to get to play cowboy. We have a lot more cattle to brand."

She wasn't kidding. For the remainder of the afternoon, they worked non-stop. And Cru and Penny didn't make as good of a team as she and Dylan had. Cru made more than a few mistakes she had to correct before he got the hang of it. With little sleep the night before, he was dead on his feet by the time they were finished for the day. Penny, on the other hand, looked energized. Like she could brand another hundred head.

On the ride back to the ranch, she maneuvered Severus next to the cutting horse she'd swapped Cru for. He thought she was going to talk about how the branding had gone. Instead, she said something completely different.

"Knock, knock."

Even as tired as he was, he couldn't help smiling. "Who's there?"

"Cows go."

"Cows go who?"

"No, silly. Cows go moo."

He tipped back his head and laughed, and she joined in. Cru forgot all about his sore shoulder and his tired muscles. He was a teenager again riding next to a sweet girl who told silly jokes. And for the first time in a long time, he didn't feel like a lone balloon floating through the sky.

It scared the hell out of him.

# CHAPTER TWELVE

"PERSONALLY, I THOUGHT THE HER-
OINE was a complete idiot. I mean why
would she choose to run off to Paris when she
could've married that nice guy Neil who owned
the butcher shop?" Luanne Riddell, who never
seemed to like the books chosen by the Simple
Ladies' Book Club, shook her head in disgust.
"Makes absolutely no sense to me whatsoever. She
could've gotten any cut of meat she wanted whenever she wanted. A girl can't ask for more than
that."

Penny glanced at Emma Johansen and they both
rolled their eyes as Raynelle Coffman jumped into
the discussion. "Having a thick-cut Porterhouse
steak for supper isn't everything, Luanne. Poor
Rebecca had already made a tragic mistake with
one man. She didn't want to rush into a relationship with another—no matter how good he was
with a butcher's knife. Take me, for example." She
picked up one of the little hot dogs baked in cres-
cent roll dough that the hostess Maureen Fulton

had made and popped it into her mouth. All the women in Maureen's family room waited patiently for Raynelle to finishing eating and continue. "After Donny Joe up and left me, I could've married Mickey Dennis, but I chose not to."

"Mickey Dennis?" Sadie asked.

"Remember, he was that truck driver from Amarillo who used to deliver Ding Dongs to the Simple Market. The man was crazy about me and proposed after the third date. But instead of saying yes, I decided to spread my wings like Rebecca and experience life."

Luanne snorted. "There is a big difference between a butcher who owns his own shop and a truck driver who delivers Ding Dongs, Raynelle. And just how have you experienced life? You haven't even been out of the state of Texas."

"I have too. I went to Texarkana to visit my Aunt Lucy just last summer."

"That's still Texas! Where do you think the Tex comes from?"

Jolene Applegate, one of the quieter book club members, spoke in a soft voice. "Well, I guess that would depend on what side your aunt lives on. If she lives on the east side, it would be Arkansas."

"And going to Arkansas is not really the same as going to Paris, France, Jolie." Luanne jumped up. "Just forget it. There's no talking to some senseless people. I'm going to get myself more chips and queso dip."

"Get me some while you're at it, Lulu," Raynelle said. "Sadie makes the best queso dip in the county."

"Will do, sugar." Luanne sent her a big smile as if she hadn't just called Raynelle senseless.

When she was gone, Maureen turned to Penny. "You haven't said much tonight, Penny. What did you think about the book?"

"I'm afraid I only got to chapter five. I've been a little busy with spring branding, although we're all finished now. So next month I shouldn't have any trouble getting the book read."

"Sounds like you got it done early this year."

They *had* finished the branding early. Thanks to Cru, Lucas, and Chester. Despite Penny's concerns, the two old cowboys had proven they could hold their own in a saddle. And even out of the saddle, they seemed to be holding their own. Lucas got around much better now that he had the boot—Raul had even made him a special stirrup—and Chester had agreed to go to the doctor's about cataract surgery. Except for a late afternoon nap under a shade tree, they worked from sunup to sundown. The ranch hands said Chester and Lucas even stayed up late some nights, regaling them with stories about their rodeoing days.

The only one who didn't seem to be thriving on the Gardener Ranch was Cru. The carefree, charming bad boy had become a withdrawn, quiet cowboy. He didn't offer to help her tag and brand again and instead herded with Chester or Lucas. When the long day was over, he headed to the bunkhouse and stayed there until the following morning. She should be thankful he was keeping his distance, but instead she missed his teasing remarks and flirtatious smiles.

She knew his melancholy mood had to do with the document she'd found in the barn. He must've discovered it in the charred rubble of Chester and Lucas's house. Is that what had made him pass out? Had he just discovered his mother had left him in a bus station? The thought made Penny feel even more sympathetic towards him.

"I bet your daddy is happy the branding's over," Raynelle said, pulling Penny's thoughts away from Cru.

"He sure is." In fact, her father was happier than he'd been in a long time. She'd thought he'd be rude to Chester and Lucas. But he'd actually been cordial to their guests—or as cordial as Hank Gardener could be. She figured his happiness had to do with getting the branding done early and with Clint coming out to the ranch for the summer. She was happy too about her nephew coming, but she was also worried.

She hadn't told Evie that Cru was staying at the ranch. She worried that if she did, her sister would go back on her bargain with their father and Hank would then kick Chester and Lucas out. Which was the same reason she hadn't pushed Evie to tell Cru about Clint.

But as soon as the summer was over and Chester and Lucas had left, Penny was going to have a long talk with her sister. Cru was still cocky, but he wasn't a carefree, irresponsible bad boy. He'd worked his tail off the last couple weeks on the ranch and refused to take pay. He watched over Lucas and Chester like a mother hen and had collected money from the other Double Diamond boys to help buy materials to rebuild their house. Maybe he wouldn't have been a good father when he was fifteen, but Penny knew he would be a good father now. And she was going to do everything in her power to make sure Evie told him the truth.

The book discussion continued. And while Luanne thought the heroine was stupid for leaving the butcher, most everyone else agreed she had guts to travel to another country by herself. Which started Suzie Dotson talking about her trip to Mexico and the bad case of diarrhea her husband got. After Suzie finished her story, Maureen asked who wanted blueberry crisp. Sadie, who had started the book club, hopped up to help her. She returned a few minutes later with two plates of blueberry crisp. One she handed to Emma and the other she gave Penny. Penny's portion was twice as big with two scoops of ice cream instead of one. Even at book club, Sadie made sure she was well fed.

"Thanks, Sadie," she said. "But this is a little much."

"Nonsense. You've been working yourself to a frazzle lately and need the extra calories. You also need to quit worrying about everyone else and worry about yourself for a change. I can't remember the last time you did something fun like go to the movies or dancing."

"She's right," Emma said as she took a bite of

her ice cream. "You worry about your sister, your nephew, and your daddy. And now you're worrying about Lucas and Chester and getting their new house built."

"With good reason," she said. "Cru and his friends are willing to put up the money to rebuild Chester and Lucas's house and we have plenty of volunteers for a house raising, but the two stubborn old men flat refuse to take any charity from anyone."

"It's hard to change stubborn men's minds." Emma gave her a pointed look. "And even stubborn women's. You need to think about yourself once in a while, Pen. You're all work and no play." Her eyes lit up. "Hey, what about if we stop by Cotton-Eyed Joe's tonight after book club. They have a new band playing with a lead singer who Mary Beth says looks just like a young Tim McGraw."

Penny didn't feel much like dancing. She felt like going back to the ranch and checking in on Chester and Lucas . . . and maybe Cru. But before she could make her excuses, Sadie cut in. "That sounds like a wonderful idea, Emma. A couple of margaritas and some line dancing is just what Penny needs."

With Sadie on Emma's side, Penny knew there was no way to successfully argue. It was better to concede with stipulations. "Okay. But just for an hour."

Emma took a big bite of blueberry crisp and smiled. "Of course we'll just stay an hour."

Cotton-Eyed Joe's was always busy on Friday nights, but this Friday it was more crowded than usual. Penny and Emma had to squeeze their way through the crowd just to get to the bar to order a drink. On their way through, everyone and their brother stopped them to talk about the different names they'd come up with for Simple. Each one was more ludicrous than the next.

"Cowpoke, Texas?" Emma said when they finally made it to the bar. "Are you kidding me?"

"It's better than Boss Hog or Tractor." Penny glanced around. "This was a bad idea. Let's come back tomorrow night when it's less crowded."

Emma swatted her arm. "Would you hush up? The more the merrier, I say. And it's going to get even merrier when we get a drink." She yelled to the bartender above the Florida Georgia Line song the band was playing. "Two margaritas, Davy!"

Penny tried to get the bartender's attention to change the order, but he'd already walked away. "Darn it, Emma. You know what tequila does to me."

"I sure do. I'll never forget you ripping off your shirt and swinging it over your head when the Dallas Cowboys scored that touchdown. Every frat boy in the bar was praying 'the boyz' would score again so they'd get to see more of your 'girls.' You're damned lucky the Cowboys were having a bad year. Of course, I wouldn't have let you strip off more than your shirt and shorts."

"Gee, thanks. You're a good friend."

"Damn straight, I am. You need to unwind a little and release that tight rein you keep on life. And if the only way to make that happen is to fill you full of tequila, so be it." Emma climbed up on the bottom rung of a barstool and peeked over everyone's heads before she climbed back down with a scowl on her face. "Mary Beth doesn't know what the heck she's talking about. The lead singer doesn't look anything like Tim McGraw—young or old."

Once they got their margaritas, they pushed their way back through the crowd looking for a table. Fortunately, Don Webber, who everyone called Duck, and his brother Rory had to leave because Duck's wife had called and told him to get his butt home or else. So they gave their table to Penny and Emma.

"Poor Duck," Emma said as they sat down. "The man can't take a pee without his wife finding out and getting on him. Just because Brandy was homecoming queen, she thinks her husband should bow down and kiss her butt."

"I don't think Duck minds." Penny took a sip of margarita. It went down nice and smooth. "Even after four kids, Brandy has a great butt."

"And a great everything else." Emma took a big drink of margarita. "Bitch."

Penny laughed and nodded in agreement as she took another sip. "Although you should talk."

"I don't have a great anything. My boobs are too small and my butt non-existent."

"Who cares about boobs and butts when you have mile-long legs and gorgeous blond hair?"

"I'll concede the legs." Emma grabbed a hank of her thick hair, which was pulled up in a ponytail. "But there is nothing gorgeous about this horse's mane that frizzes up like a Brillo pad in the slightest humidity. I can't even wear it down it's so bad. I'm thinking about cutting it and dying it blue like Raynelle's."

Penny took another sip of margarita. "If you dye it blue and I dye mine silver we'd be all set for high school football season." She pumped her fist. "Go, Spartans!"

"Go, Spartans!" Emma echoed before she waved down a passing waitress and ordered them more margaritas.

After two margaritas, Penny forgot all about going home. After three, she and Emma were having the best time ever. After four, they headed out to the dance floor where they danced three line dances—badly—and then attempted to two-step with Emma leading and Penny following. Which resulted in stepped-on toes and a whole lot of laughter. Guys tried to cut in, but Emma and Penny were having too much fun to let a man in the mix. Margarita-filled bladders finally broke up their dance party.

When Penny had trouble getting out of the bathroom stall, she realized just how drunk she was. "Friend! I'm locked in!" she hollered to Emma in the next stall.

"Don't worry, honey. I'm a comin'." The toilet next door flushed and suddenly Emma's head appeared beneath the stall. She shimmed under like a soldier along the front lines, then grabbed onto Penny's legs and pulled herself up. Once she was standing, they fell into each other and cracked up laughing.

"I think we're drunk," Emma said.

"I know we are. I told you we shouldn't have had that last round of margaritas."

"What do you mean? You bought it."

"Oh yeah." Penny giggled.

It took both of their alcohol-soaked brains to get out of the stall. After a water fight while washing their hands, they hooked arms and headed back to their table. On the way past the bar, Emma came to a sudden stop.

"I spy with my little eye a super hot bad boy that makes me sigh."

Penny followed her gaze and saw Cru sitting at the end of the bar nursing a beer. His cowboy hat was tipped back, and his dark hair fell over his forehead in a cute, sexy way that sent Penny's tummy to tumbling. Or maybe it was her heart that went tumbling because he looked so lost sitting there all alone. Just like a lost little boy in a bus station.

Like iron filings to a magnet, she moved toward him. When she was directly behind him, she placed her hand on his shoulder. Lucas had told her Cru had gotten his stitches out and was good as new, but she couldn't help caressing the spot with her fingers. He turned, and she forgot all about stitches as she got lost in his spring-green eyes. Before she could find her way out, Emma stepped up.

"So here's the town hero." She sent him a flirty

smile. "I heard all about you saving Chester and Lucas from the fire, Cru Cassidy."

"If I were a true hero, I would've kept a closer eye on Lucas and they'd still have their house."

"On the bright side, at least you don't have to worry about fixin' the toilets anymore."

A smile lit Cru's face. A smile Penny hadn't seen in what felt like forever. And it annoyed the heck out of her that Emma was the one on the receiving end of such beauty. Before she could stop it, the thought popped right out of her mouth.

"Why don't you smile at me anymore?"

His gaze flickered over to her, and his smile faded. "Excuse me?"

"Smile at me." She used two fingers to tip up the corners of his mouth. But as soon as she removed them, his lips drooped into a frown. As did his eyebrows.

"How much have you had to drink?"

"Too much, obviously," Emma said. "Good God, Pen, would you stop mauling the man?" She winked at Cru. "What she's trying to say is that your smiles are flat-out sexy, and we'd like to see more of them. In fact, have you ever thought about having a threesome?"

Even Drunk Penny knew that had crossed over the line. "Emma!"

"What? I wasn't talking about in bed. I was talking about on the dance floor."

Cru laughed. "No, I can't say as I've ever had a threesome—in bed or on the dance floor. It's certainly something I'd like to try, just not tonight. And from the looks of things, I don't think you ladies should be trying it tonight either." He glanced at Penny. "Did you drive here?"

"Yes," Emma chimed in. "But don't worry. I won't let her drive home. I'll call my dope of a partner to come get us. He'll jump at the chance when he finds out I'm with Penny."

A knot formed between Cru's dark eyebrows. Penny reached out to smooth it away, but he caught her wrist and stopped her. "I'll drive you." Holding on to her wrist, he got up, and then he steered her and Emma through the crowd and out the door to his truck.

"Shotgun!" Emma yelled as soon as Cru pulled open the passenger door. Which left Penny in the back seat. Something she wasn't real thrilled about. Nor was she thrilled when Cru buckled her in like a toddler.

"I'm not a kid," she grumbled as he pulled the seatbelt across her lap. His gaze found hers as his hand brushed her hip.

"Believe me, I know that."

Since she lived in town, Cru took Emma home first. On the way, Emma chattered like a magpie, leaving Penny to feel like a mute spare tire. "What happened to your fancy red car?"

"I traded it in for this," he said.

Penny was surprised. She knew he'd gotten a new truck, but she hadn't thought he'd traded in the Porsche for it. She'd thought he'd left the Porsche at Chester and Lucas's.

"You traded it for this?" Emma said. "I like a big

ol' truck as much as any Texas girl, but a used truck sure isn't worth a pretty candy-apple-red Porsche that could probably go from zero to sixty in the blink of an eye."

"Sometimes going fast isn't all it's cracked up to be," Cru said. "Sometimes it's better to take your time."

"I do love a man who knows how to take his time," Emma said in a sultry voice, and Penny reached between the seat and the door and pinched her arm. "Oww!" She swiveled around and shot her a mean glare. "What was that for, Penelope Anne Gardener?"

"For ordering me that second margarita," she lied.

"And here's for ordering the third and fourth." Emma reached back and pinched her leg. They got into a pinching war until Cru cut in.

"I hate to break up a good cat fight, but which house is yours, Emma?"

"The hot pink one. I made a little tiny mistake and ordered the wrong color paint for one of our customers. To keep Boone from finding out I had to act like the ten gallons of pink paint were mine. Thus, the Barbie Dream house."

Cru laughed, and Penny scowled. She didn't like Emma making Cru laugh. And she didn't like him getting out and opening Emma's door. Or taking her arm when she swayed—no doubt on purpose—and helping her up the path to her house. Once they got to the porch it was too dark to see what was going on. But Penny didn't doubt for a second that Emma was trying to get a goodnight kiss.

She rolled down her window and stuck her head out. "Any time this week!" A few seconds later, Cru came down the steps of the porch. When he got into the truck, her drunk tongue wouldn't be still. "So did you kiss her?" She thumped her forehead with her palm. Or tried to. She missed a little and hit her eye instead. "Stupid question. Of course you kissed her. You kiss every girl who comes within a mile of you."

He did a U-turn and headed toward the highway that led out of town. "Not every girl. Just the ones who are willing."

She snorted. "And every girl is willing, aren't they? Of course they are. Who could resist your pretty green eyes and your dimpled smile and your teasing charm?"

"You're drunk, Penny. It's probably best if you don't say anything that might embarrass you later."

"You're right. I am drunk, but I refuse to shut up. I'm tired of being sweet Penelope Anne who keeps her mouth shut and never speaks up for what she wants. Sweet Penelope who always takes the back seat." She took off her seatbelt and crawled over the console.

"What are you doing?"

She ignored the question and fell awkwardly into the bucket seat with her boots still draped over the console. "Sweet Penelope Anne is taking what she wants." She needed to shut up. She really needed to shut up. But instead she spoke the words she had no business speaking.

"Because no matter how hard I tried not to, I still want you, Cru Cassidy."

# CHAPTER THIRTEEN

CRU KEPT HIS GAZE PINNED on the high-way and away from the sexy disheveled woman leaning so close to him that he could smell the tequila and lime on her breath. "That's just the drink talking. You don't want me, Penny."

"Don't tell me what I want, Cru. I've spent all of my life keeping my own needs and desire hidden so I wouldn't rock the boat. After my mother died, I put on a brave face so no one would know exactly how hurt I was. When my sister and daddy fought over anything and everything, I became the mediator when I really want to just cover my ears and tell them to shut the hell up. And when Evie started liking you, I didn't tell her that I liked you first. I didn't tell her that you were mine before you were hers. But you were mine, Cru. You were mine the first time you rescued me."

He should be shouting hallelujahs that a few margaritas had done away with the sister pact and he could finally ease the desire that had been rid-ing him hard ever since he'd come back to Simple.

But even with the sister pact out of the way, there was something else keeping him from pulling over and taking what was being offered. His conscience. Not only because Penny was obviously drunk and he'd never taken advantage of an inebriated girl, but also because in the last few weeks, he'd come to realize Penny wasn't for him. He was big city. She was small town. He couldn't stay put for longer than a few months at a time. She didn't want to live anywhere but on her beloved ranch. He was an irresponsible playboy who cared about no one. She was a responsible do-gooder who cared about everyone.

Every ranch hand had a story to tell about her caring nature. She'd loaned Sam money to fix his truck when it had broken down. She'd stopped by the hospital every day to see Billy's mother when she had cancer. She'd talked her father into hiring Raul and helped him and his family become American citizens. She'd hassled Cru every day about keeping his stitches clean and bandaged until he'd gotten them out and made sure Chester and Lucas drank plenty of water while they were working so they wouldn't get dehydrated. It was like she felt responsible for the entire world.

And damned if Cru could take advantage of someone with a heart that big. Which was why he'd decided to keep his distance from her. Penny deserved to be with someone as good as she was. Not an irresponsible drifter who had no intentions of staying. But it was hard to keep his distance when Penny had lost all her inhibitions. He almost jumped out of his seat when she pressed her finger to his bottom lip.

"Did you know, when I was a kid, I used to keep track of how many times you smiled? I wrote it down in my diary every single night. Along with everything you ever said to me. My goal was to get you to smile at least fifty times a day. I even bought a joke book to help me achieve my goal." She ran her finger along his bottom lip. Cru instantly hardened beneath the fly of his jeans.

Damn. Why hadn't he just let Boone drive her home?

He knew the answer. Jealousy. The same jealousy that ate through his gut every time Dylan or any other ranch hand got within a few feet of her. And he didn't know where this jealous streak came from. He had never let jealousy affect him before and he had no business letting it affect him now.

Ignoring the desire pressing against his zipper like a sore tooth that needed filling, he removed her finger from his lip. "So that explains all those knock-knock jokes."

"Knock, knock."

He glanced over to see her watching him with sultry eyes. He swallowed hard and looked back at the road. "Who's there?"

"Kiss."

He knew where this was headed and refused to reply with, "Kiss who?" But that didn't stop her from answering as if he had.

"Kiss me." She leaned over and ran her tongue along his earlobe in a slide of wet heat that had him veering off the road. The truck flattened a good twenty yards of weeds and wildflowers before he brought it to a halt.

He turned in his seat to tell her this wasn't a good idea, but as soon as he opened his mouth, her lips covered his. She tasted like tequila and innocence, a potent combination. At first taste, he felt as intoxicated as she was.

There was a desperate franticness in the way she kissed him, like a kid eating ice cream before it all melted in the heat of the sun. She sucked and pulled at his lips like she couldn't get enough. Her neediness sent his desire spiraling, but he ignored his need and tried to push her away. She wasn't having it. She unbuckled her seat belt and crawled right over the console into his lap.

She fit perfectly. Her butt nestled against his hard-on and her soft breasts seared a hole in his chest. He desperately wanted to tug open two snaps of her western shirt and slip his hand inside her bra to cradle the supple fullness of her breasts. Desperately wanted to feel her nipple drilling into his palm before he pushed down her bra and lowered his head for a deep taste of her sweet flesh. Instead, he pulled away from the kiss and spoke the hardest words he'd ever had to say.

"No, Penny. We can't do this."

"Cru," she whispered his name like a prayer. "Please." The pleading in her voice strengthened his resolve. Penny wasn't just pleading for a night of hot sex. She was pleading for something more. She might not know what it was, but he did. She was pleading for a man to love her like she deserved to be loved. As much as Cru wanted to be that man, he knew he wasn't.

He lifted her and set her back in her seat. "I need to get you home." He took a deep uneven breath before he put the truck into drive and pulled back out on the road.

"But I don't want to go home."

"I know what you want, Penny. And I can't give it to you. I can't give it to any woman."

She flopped back in the seat and snorted. "As if I believe that. You've given sex to plenty of women, Cru Cassidy. Including my sister!"

Once again, he almost drove off the road. He corrected his steering and glanced over at her in shock. "Your sister? You think I had sex with your sister?"

"I don't think. I know. The proof is my fourteen-year-old nephew." Her eyes widened as much as Cru's did, and she clamped a hand over her mouth as he tried to recover from the bomb she'd just dropped.

Too stunned to drive, he pulled over to the shoulder and turned to her. "You think I got Evie pregnant?"

She squeezed her eyes closed and spoke through her fingers. "Oh my God, what am I doing? I almost had sex with my nephew's father." Her face lost all color and her eyes popped open as she fumbled with the door handle.

"What are you doing?"

She didn't answer as she opened the door and

jumped out. She left the door open, and he watched as she bent over and threw up in the wildflowers growing by the road.

He leaned back in the seat and ran a hand through his hair as he tried to digest what she'd just told him. Penny hadn't just thought he kissed Evie. She thought he'd had sex with Evie. And not just that: she thought he'd gotten her pregnant. No wonder she'd hated him when he first got there. But how had she come to that conclusion? The only answer seemed to be Evie.

He grabbed the bottle of water he always kept in the cup holder and got out. By the time he made it around the truck, Penny had stopped throwing up and was sitting on the ground with her head and arms resting on her bent knees.

"You okay?" he asked.

"No. I'm dying."

"I wish I could tell you that you'll feel better in the morning. But you'll probably feel worse."

She moaned. "Then shoot me now and put me out of my misery."

"Here." He held out the bottle. "Drink some water. It will help."

She lifted her head and accepted the bottle. After she had taken a few sips, she spoke. "Thank you. Not just for the water, but also for driving me home. I'm sure you didn't plan to spend your Friday night watching a woman throw up . . . or being mauled by her."

"I never mind being mauled by a beautiful woman. And I've had my fair share of tequila nights where I've done some embarrassing things."

"I'm sure you never had to force yourself on a woman." She screwed the lid on the bottle. "I'm sorry. It was a huge mistake."

"Because you really didn't want to or because I had sex with your sister and got her pregnant?"

Her gaze snapped up to him. "Yet another reason I shouldn't drink tequila. It makes me say things I have no business saying."

"Who told you I had sex with Evie?"

She got to her feet. She weaved a little and he took her arm and steadied her. Her gaze locked with his. "No one had to tell me, Cru. I saw you kiss her. And I overheard you bragging to the other boys about how you had sex with her."

He *had* bragged about having sex with Evie. But it had been a lie. He hadn't even made it to second base with her. After one chaste kiss, she'd pushed him away before he could get another. It had been a major blow to his fifteen-year-old super-sized ego, so he'd lied to the other boys. It looked like he hadn't been the only one lying.

"And you asked Evie and she told you it was me?" he asked.

"She wouldn't tell anyone who it was. She knew how much my father hated the Double Diamond boys and she didn't want him to find out and do something that would get him tossed in jail. Or try to get revenge on Chester and Lucas for bringing you there in the first place."

So it was a Double Diamond boy who had gotten Evie pregnant? He couldn't believe it. He'd been the only boy after Evie. What kind of game was Penny's sister playing? Whatever it was, it pissed him off. Not only was Penny's father a jerk, her sister was too. He wanted to tell Penny the truth, but he decided it would be best if he waited until she was sober. She was still unsteady on her feet and probably wouldn't even remember their conversation tomorrow.

"Come on. Let's get you home."

They didn't talk the rest of the way to the Gardener Ranch. Cru was busy trying to figure out which one of his friends had gotten Evie pregnant, and Penny looked like she had fallen asleep. Or more likely passed out. Once he pulled up in front of the porch, he jumped out to open her door. He thought he might have to carry her inside, but by the time he got around the truck, she was getting out on her own. He took her arm to help her and her gaze lifted to his. "Did you love her?"

He should lie. Keeping Evie between them would be for the best. But damned if he could lie to those clear blue eyes. "No, I didn't love Evie. I've never loved any woman."

"Because your mom left you in a bus station?"

He felt like someone had stripped him naked and shown all his imperfections to the world. His face heated with humiliation. "Who told you that? Chester? Lucas?"

She stared back at him, her eyes wide and filled with sympathy. "I found the Double Diamond Boys' Ranch questionnaire in the barn."

All the pieces fell together. She'd found the questionnaire the same day she'd invited him to the ranch. She hadn't asked him here to watch out for Chester and Lucas. She'd invited him here because she felt sorry for the poor orphan kid whose mother had left him at the bus station. He couldn't help feeling embarrassed and angry.

"I'm not some fuckin' three-legged dog that needs your sympathy or a home, Penny," he snapped. "I've done just fine in my life without a mom. In fact, I don't even remember her."

It was a lie. He remembered everything about his mother. Her long, dark hair that brushed his cheek when she leaned down to give him a goodnight kiss. The sparkle in her green eyes when he did something to make her laugh. The lyrical sound of her voice when she sang him lullabies. But mostly, he remembered the feel of her arms when she gave him a long, tight hug before he went into the stall to use the bathroom.

And he remembered the desperation and fear he felt when he came out and she was gone. Penny was right. He didn't trust any woman with his heart because he never wanted to feel that pain again. But if he could trust someone, it would be Penny. And she didn't deserve to be snapped at just because she'd felt sympathy for the four-year-old boy he once was.

"I'm sorry," he said. "I just don't like to talk about the past." He held onto her as they walked to the porch. When they reached the steps, she turned to him and sent him a quizzical look.

"Do you really think you're as cute as Trixie?"

He laughed, but his laughter died when she reached up and brushed a strand of hair off his forehead. "You're wrong. Everyone needs a mom, Cru." Before he could reply, she climbed the steps and disappeared inside.

Her words stuck with him as walked back to his truck. Once inside, he glanced at the glove box. He should've left the letter in the Porsche when he sold it. Instead, he had pulled it out at the last minute. He hated himself for the weakness. And he hated his mother even more.

Intending to rip the letter into shreds, he opened the glove compartment and took it out. He stared at the handwriting on the front of the envelope. It had been addressed to Father Stephen but hadn't reached him until he'd been too ill to send it on to Cru. Or maybe the old priest had never planned to forward it. Maybe he'd been smart enough to know the past should be left in the past. It had been Sister Bernadette who found it when she was going through Father Stephen's things. At the funeral, she had been so excited to give it to him. The sister thought she was giving him the best gift of all when she told him his mother was looking for him and had given Father Stephen her contact information.

But the information meant nothing to Cru.

He'd stopped looking for his mother years ago.

# CHAPTER FOURTEEN

PENNY WOKE UP WITH A queasy stomach, a pounding head, and the feeling that she'd done something very wrong. As soon as she remembered what that something was, her stomach and headache took a back seat to humiliation, guilt, and fear. She was humiliated for acting like a lovesick idiot with Cru. Guilty for trying to seduce her nephew's father. And terrified her sister was going to kill her for letting the cat out of the bag.

"I hate tequila," she moaned as she rolled to her back and covered her face with a pillow. The sound of Sketcher sneakers squeaking against the wooden floor had her pulling the pillow off her face and looking at Sadie, who stood there holding a tray in her hands.

"Stop being so dramatic, Penelope Anne." Sadie set the tray on the nightstand and Penny could smell the wonderful aroma of hot coffee. "You just had some fun last night. It's not the end of the world." She walked to the window and pushed open the curtains.

The blinding sunlight that flooded in made Penny's head throb even more. It also made her realize how late it was. She sat straight up, then had to close her eyes to regain her equilibrium. "What time is it?"

"Close to ten."

Her eyes flew open. "Ten! I have a million things to do this morning." She started to swing her legs over the edge of the bed, but Sadie stopped her.

"Stay right where you are, young lady. You're in no condition to do ranch work today."

"But I need to help Dylan fix the north fence and the vet is coming to check out that sick calf and I talked Chester into going to the ophthalmologist for his cataracts and his appointment is this afternoon."

"I'll be happy to take Chester to his appointment. Dylan can get one of the other ranch hands to help him with the fence. And I told your father you're not feeling well so I'm sure he'll take care of the vet."

Penny flopped back. She really didn't feel well. She groaned and covered her face with a pillow again. Sadie removed it and sat down on the edge of the bed.

"Here, have some coffee. It will help with that margarita hangover." She picked up the steaming mug from the tray and held it out.

Penny sat up and took it, sighing when the aroma of the coffee filled her nose. "How do you know it's a margarita hangover? I could've been doing shots."

"You know how word travels in a small town. Millie Stanton called me to go over the minutes of the last garden club meeting and mentioned her son saw you and Emma downing margaritas last night at Cotton-Eyed Joe's." Penny rolled her eyes and Sadie swatted her leg. "She wasn't gossiping maliciously. She agrees with me that it's about time you enjoyed life instead of spending all your time working the ranch."

"I enjoyed myself a little too much last night." As she sipped her coffee, the events of the night before paraded through her mind like the vacation videos her Grandfather and Grandmother Myers used to make her sit through, and it wasn't pretty. She cringed.

"It couldn't have been that bad," Sadie said. "Although I was a little concerned when I heard you left with Cru Cassidy. Is there something going on between you two?"

The night before proved there was plenty going on between them. Or at least on her end. All it had taken was a few margaritas for her to forget all about his relationship with Evie and return to that thirteen-year-old girl who made a fool out of herself over him. If he hadn't put a stop to things, she had little doubt she'd feel even guiltier right now.

"Nothing's going on between me and Cru," she lied. "He just drove me home because I'd had too much to drink."

Sadie sent her a knowing look. "Do you think I was born yesterday? I've seen the way you look at him. It's the same way you looked at him when you were thirteen."

Penny stared at her in surprise. "You knew I had a crush on Cru?"

"Of course I knew. Anyone with eyes could see it."

"Daddy and Evie didn't."

"I'm not so sure about Evie. But your daddy has blinders on where you're concerned. You're his baby girl. The one who worships the ground he walks on. He can't see that ever changing."

"That might've been true when I was a little girl, but I don't worship the ground he walks on now. We argue all the time about how to run the ranch."

"Argue. But if you notice, you're always the one who gives in."

She opened her mouth to deny it, but then realized Sadie was right. "Just because I don't want to get in a major fight like Evie that doesn't mean I worship him. I just respect him as my father and a man who knows a lot more about ranching than I do."

"You don't give yourself enough credit, Penny. I think you've long since earned a say in how this ranch is run. But I figure you'll stand your ground when it's something that really matters to you. I just hope that something isn't Cru Cassidy."

She tried to ease Sadie's mind . . . and her own. "I might've had a crush on him when I was a kid, but every girl has a teenage crush. If you catch me looking at him now, it's just because . . . well, he's a good-looking man. Can't a girl notice a hot cowboy?"

"If you were another woman, I'd think nothing of it. But you've never taken note of hot cowboys before and there have been plenty of them around. Dylan Matheson is a good example. He's one fine-looking young man and you don't give him a second glance. Nor have you given any other man a second look. I can count on one hand how many times you've gone out on a date in the last year."

Penny set her coffee on the nightstand. "Ranching is hard work. I have enough to worry about without adding a man to the mix."

"Well, if you didn't want to add a man to the mix, why did you invite Cru to stay here? I can see inviting Chester and Lucas. They're our neighbors and they lost their home. But Cru is a big boy. He could've stayed in town at Dixon's Boardinghouse."

Penny was surprised. It was the first time Sadie had ever been anything but hospitable. "Are you saying you don't want Cru here?"

"I'm saying I don't want you hurt. And Cru Cassidy is the type of man who leaves a trail of broken hearts in his wake. If anyone should know that, you should. Especially after what happened to Evie."

"So Evie *did* tell you that Cru is Clint's father."

The stunned look on Sadie's face made Penny realize she'd just put her foot in her mouth. "Where in the world did you get that crazy notion?"

"But I thought that's why you said especially after what happened to Evie."

"I was talking about your heart being broken when Cru leaves like Evie's was when her boy left her. But that boy wasn't Cru Cassidy."

Penny felt like she'd been tossed off a horse and had all the wind knocked out of her. She stared at Sadie. "But Cru was the only boy who chased after her that summer."

"He might've chased after her, but you should know your sister never did like to be the one getting chased. She wanted to be the chaser. And Cru Cassidy wasn't the boy she set her sights on."

Penny felt like she was still asleep and dreaming. "But all the facts point to Cru. She was in love with him. I know she was. When we talked about him, she always agreed that he was funny and charming and handsome. And she kissed him. I saw it with my own two eyes."

Sadie sent her an exasperated look. "Do we need to have that sex talk again? Because kissing isn't how you make babies, honey. And while Evie might've agreed with you that Cru was handsome and charming, she didn't think he was as handsome and charming as another boy."

"But who could be more handsome and charming than Cru?"

Sadie shook her head. "And you said you weren't infatuated with him. You're so infatuated you think every other woman is too. But believe me when I tell you, Evie was not in love with Cru."

If she was going to believe anyone, it would be Sadie. An overwhelming rush of joy filled her. "It isn't Cru."

Sadie released an exasperated sigh. "That look on your face is exactly what I was afraid of. Evie falling for a Double Diamond boy is more than enough. I won't have you falling for one too. Those boys didn't stay at the ranch because they were a bunch of sweet teenagers who wanted to learn how to cowboy. They were there because they had deep emotional scars and had gotten into some kind of trouble. And as much as I hope all those boys grew up to became law-abiding citizens and successful adults, I'm pretty sure that some of them are still dealing with those emotional scars. Like Cru Cassidy. You can take one look at him and know that boy is still lost."

She couldn't help defending Cru. "He has good reason to be lost, Sadie. He grew up in a children's home after his mother left him in a bus station when he was only four years old. Four years old." Her eyes filled with tears as she remembered how adamant Cru had been when he said he cared nothing about his mother. But his anger proved he cared too much about her.

Sadie shook her head before she pulled Penny into her arms. "You're just like your mama. She had a heart the size of Texas and wanted to save every lost soul she met. That's why she chose your father. If you think he's hard now, it's nothing to what he was before your mother got ahold of him. But underneath his gruff exterior is a good man." She drew back, her eyes still sad. "I'm not so sure about Cru. His past might be too much for him to overcome. And I'd hate for you to find that out after you've already invested your heart. Although with the way you look at him, I'm not so sure that hasn't already happened."

"It hasn't." She didn't know if she was trying to convince Sadie or herself. "I'm not a wide-eyed thirteen-year-old anymore. I know Cru isn't the type of man who wants to settle down. But that doesn't mean he's not a good man. Look how much he cares for Chester and Lucas. And how much he's helped on the ranch. While I'm not going to offer him my heart, I am going to offer him my friendship. He deserves at least that after I falsely believed he was Clint's father. And the entire misunderstanding is all Evie's fault. It's time she stopped hiding the truth and owned up to it. If not to Daddy, at least to Clint." She thought Sadie would agree and was surprised when she didn't.

"I don't think that's a good idea. Sometimes it's best to let sleeping dogs lie."

"How can you say that? Clint deserves to know who his father is."

Sadie got up from the bed and walked to the window. "Even if his father doesn't want to know him?"

"His father knows about Clint? But Evie acted like she didn't tell him."

Sadie turned around. "She didn't. I did. When Clint was around one, I contacted his father. At first, he was angry Evie hadn't told him. But later, he called me and thanked me for letting him know. He said his son would be better off not having someone like him as a father. But he promised to send money for Evie when he could. He kept his promise. I started receiving money like clockwork.

At first, it was just a couple twenties in an envelope every other week, but gradually the cash turned into checks in amounts much larger."

Penny stared at her. "Why didn't Evie tell me she was getting money? Is that how she paid for college and the house in Abilene?"

"From what she says, she hasn't touched any of the money. I think she was angry he didn't care enough about Clint to come back, and maybe she was also angry that he didn't care enough about her. The money is in a savings account she plans to give Clint for his college. Although the amount that's accumulated will cover a lot more than college."

It was shocking news and Penny couldn't help feeling hurt Evie hadn't confided in her. Sadie must've read her expression because she walked back over to the bed, sat down, and took her hand. "I wouldn't be too mad at Evie. She kept the secret not only so you wouldn't have to lie to your father, but also because she knew that if your father found out I'd kept Clint's daddy's identity from him, he'd fire me."

"But I don't understand. Clint's father sends money, but he doesn't want to meet his own son."

"It's like I was saying. Some men's scars are just too deep to heal. And as much as we want to heal them, we can't." She pulled Penny in for another hug. "Be friends with Cru, but please protect your heart, honey." She got to her feet. "Now I need to go start lunch for a crew of hungry cowboys."

Penny threw back the covers and got up. "Just let

me take a quick shower and I'll help you."

"I appreciate the offer, but a nice long shower is exactly what you need to get over that hangover."

Sadie was right. The shower did make her feel better. The hot water soothed her achy muscles and the steam cleared her head. But it was the truth about Cru that made her tummy feel all buoyant with happiness. She was thrilled Cru wasn't Clint's father, but confused he hadn't told her the truth last night. Of course, maybe he had and she'd been too drunk to remember. Or still too infatuated with Cru to believe any woman would choose another man over him.

She thought back to the summer and tried to remember it without the haze of a schoolgirl's crush. Despite the one kiss, Cru and Evie hadn't acted like a couple of lovesick teenagers. There had been no hand holding or flirtatious teasing. In fact, now that she thought about it, she had spent more time with Cru than Evie had. But who had Evie spent time with? She couldn't remember seeing her sister with any of the boys. Evie had spent most of her time reading in the old abandoned shack on the Double Diamond Ranch. At least, that's what she'd told Penny she was doing. Now she had to wonder if Evie had been alone at the shack. It was something she planned to find out. There were going to be no more secrets between the Gardener sisters.

Unfortunately, when she got out of the shower and called her sister, Evie didn't answer. She left a quick message before she got dressed.

In the kitchen, she found Sadie wrapping burritos in aluminum foil as she sang along with the radio. Sadie had a beautiful singing voice and sang solos at church almost every Sunday. Penny's voice wasn't nearly as good, but she joined in with a George Strait song as she helped Sadie finish. As Sadie cut a pan of cherry crumble bars into squares, Penny snagged one for breakfast and munched on it while they put the others in plastic baggies. Each bag had two bars, except for one Sadie put three in.

"Is that for Daddy?" Penny asked. "I thought the doctor told him to cut back on his sweets."

"That's why I didn't pack any for him. This one is for Cru." When Penny lifted her eyebrows, Sadie shrugged. "Did you or did you not say the boy needs some extra love? I don't want you giving it to him and getting hurt, but this old mother hen can. Now let's get these packed up in the cooler with the apples and drinks so I can get going. I need to finish the laundry before I take Chester to his appointment."

"I can take Chester," Penny said. "I'm fine. And I can take lunch too. I need to check on that fence Dylan is mending anyway."

Sadie shook her head in exasperation. "I should've known you couldn't take the whole day off."

First, Penny stopped by the barn to give Raul his lunch. She found her father and Billy with him in the paddock checking out the new horse her father had purchased. The mare was an unbroken Appaloosa that seemed even more Ill-tempered than Severus. The horse was rearing and posing and putting on quite a show.

"I thought you were sick," her father said when he saw her.

"Must've been something I ate."

"Or drank," Billy said with a smirk, and she remembered he had been one of the men who tried to cut in on her and Emma last night while they were dancing.

She sent him a warning look to keep his big mouth shut, then she told them to come out to the truck to get their lunch. Once she'd passed out their food and drinks, she asked her father where Chester, Lucas, and Cru were.

"I sent them to help Dylan with the fence."

That wasn't good. She didn't know why, but for some reason Dylan and Cru had taken a dislike to each other. And as soon as she got out to the north pasture, she realized the dislike had turned ugly.

The men were on the ground fighting while Chester and Lucas cheered them on.

# CHAPTER FIFTEEN

CRU COULDN'T REMEMBER THE LAST time he'd been in a fight. He'd always been more of a lover than a fighter. But when Dylan told him to stay away from Penny, something snapped inside him, and he hauled off and threw a punch. Dylan didn't go down easy. He came back with a right hook that rang Cru's bell. From there, things escalated until they both ended up on the ground. Cru had finally gotten the upper hand and straddled Dylan when a loud shot rang out.

He glanced up and saw Penny standing there looking like Annie Oakley with a rifle resting on her hip and pointing at the sky. "That's enough," she said in a stern voice that made him smile. Anyone who knew her knew she didn't have a stern bone in her body. But since his jaw ached, his eye throbbed, and he could taste blood, he figured she might have a point. He lowered the fist he was about to throw and got to his feet, then held out a hand to help Dylan up. Dylan ignored the hand and got up by himself.

Cru turned to Penny. "Good mornin'. It looks like you survived last night."

Her cheeks blossomed with color, and she cleared her throat. "What in the world is going on here?"

"A damn good fight that would've been even better if you hadn't broken it up." Lucas handed Cru his hat before he looked at Chester. "You owe me ten dollars."

"Like hell I do, you old coot," Chester replied. "You owe me ten."

"You really do need those cataracts removed, you old fart. Cru was the one on top."

"But Dylan connected twice as many—"

Penny cut in. "You bet on the fight? You should've stopped it."

"Why would we stop a good fight?" Lucas asked. "All cowboys fight every now and again. It gets out pent up aggression." He looked at Chester. "We've had our fair share of fights, haven't we, Chess? Especially over women. Remember that little gal from Galveston? What was her name?"

"Debbie Dozer."

"Oh yeah, Little Debbie. She was sure sweeter than a store-bought snack cake. And you sure were ticked she liked me better."

Chester's eyes narrowed behind his thick glasses. "Hell, she didn't like you better. She liked me better."

"Bull hockey!" Lucas took a hobbled step closer to his brother with a fist raised.

"Whoa there." Cru stepped between them. "I think one fist fight a day is plenty." He dusted off his hat on his pant leg. Although seeing how he was covered in red dirt, it didn't help.

Penny lowered the rifle and glanced at Dylan. "What happened?"

There was a cowboy code that Chester and Lucas had taught Cru a long time ago: Cowboys didn't tattle. It seemed Dylan had learned the code as well.

"We just had a little disagreement is all." He picked up his hat. "We got the fence taken care of here, so I'll head over to the northeast corner."

Penny opened her mouth as if she wanted to further her interrogation, but then changed her mind. "There are burritos in the thermal bag and drinks in the cooler in the bed of the truck. Help yourself before you head out." She looked at Chester. "And don't forget you have a doctor's appointment this afternoon."

"I'm not lettin' some yahoo cut on my eyes," Chester snapped.

"No one is going to cut on your eyes today. You're just going in to talk to the doctor."

"Fine, but all I'm doin' is talkin'."

"You better do more than talk, you old fart," Lucas said. "You're still blind as a bat. Especially if you think Dylan won that fight. And what do you think you're doin' bettin' against one of our boys?"

"If we'd both bet on Cru, where's the fun in that? Besides, I like Dylan. He's a good kid. And you should talk about disabilities, Hopalong."

Grumbling insults back and forth, they headed to Penny's truck. When they were gone, she looked at Cru. "Do you want to tell me what happened?"

"Like Dylan said, it was just a little disagreement."

She studied him for a moment before she sighed. "Fine. I'll let it go this time. But I'd appreciate it if next time you and Dylan disagree you use words." She pulled a bandanna out of her back pocket and stepped closer. "You're bleeding." She placed a hand on the back of his neck and pressed the bandanna against his bottom lip. He couldn't stop the surge of heat that filled him.

He stepped away. "It's not a big deal. I better grab a burrito so Dylan and I can get the other fence fixed."

"I think it's best if you two stay away from each other. I'll get someone else to help Dylan. You can grab something to eat and then head back to the ranch to clean up." She pulled out her cellphone and moved away to talk.

Since he wasn't very hungry, Cru double checked the fence and gathered up his tools. He felt like an idiot. Why had he gotten angry at Dylan for asking him to stay away from Penny when that was exactly his plan? Obviously, if he couldn't have her, he didn't want anyone else to, either. But someday someone would have her. Hopefully, someone who would treat her right and give her the love she deserved. Cru couldn't help but be envious of the lucky sonofabitch.

Once he had his tools loaded up, he walked to Penny's truck. Chester and Lucas were sitting on the tailgate eating their burritos. Penny was leaning next to them sipping a Dr. Pepper. When he walked up, she handed him a foil-wrapped burrito.

"Thanks. I'll eat it on the way to the ranch." He looked at Chester and Lucas. "You two coming?"

"We can't go back until we finish those fences," Chester said. "A job's not done until it's done."

"Suit yourself." He flipped up the lid of the cooler and grabbed a Dr. Pepper before he headed to his truck.

It was a blistering hot day. On the way to the ranch, he passed the copse of trees that surrounded Mesquite Springs. A cool swim sounded much better than a hot shower, so he pulled off the road and parked. Leaving his clothes on a rock, he waded into the springs. The water was warmer than it had been a month ago. An image of Penny in wet underwear popped into his head, but he pushed it right back out and dove under.

As a teenager, he'd stayed in the springs for hours swimming and horsing around with his friends. He and the other boys had loved to swing from the rope swing and dunk each other under. Logan was the only one who didn't like horseplay, something everyone had figured out when Lincoln had grabbed Logan's feet and pulled him under. Logan had gone ballistic. He hadn't liked being touched. Not a slap on the back or a playful dunk.

A loud splash pulled him from his thoughts. He stopped swimming and treaded watering looking for the source of the sound. He noticed the rope swaying back and forth only seconds before Penny popped up in front of him, her fiery hair slicked back and her long lashes spiked with water. He was trying his best to stay away from her, but she wasn't making it easy.

"What are you doing here?" he asked.

"What does it look like I'm doing? I came for a swim."

His gaze lowered to her wet bra straps. Just below the surface of the water, he could see the shape of her bra-covered breasts. He quickly lifted his gaze. "I thought you were going to help Dylan."

"I called Billy to help him. He picked up Chester and Lucas on his way from the ranch."

"So you just decided to come swimming?"

"No. I was headed back to the ranch to talk with you when I saw your truck."

"Look, we don't need to talk any more about the fight. I give you my word it won't happen again."

She treaded water, her hands circling. "I don't want to talk about the fight. I wanted to apologize about last night."

"You had a few too many margaritas. It happens to all of us. It was no big deal, Penny." That was a lie. He'd stayed up half the night thinking about her sweet lips devouring his. And he couldn't help looking at the droplet of water that clung to her bottom lip and wishing for a repeat. Especially when she seductively sucked it off.

"I didn't come here to apologize for last night. I came here to apologize for thinking you got Evie pregnant."

"Who told you the truth? Evie?"

"It doesn't matter. What matters is that I shouldn't have accused you without having real proof."

"I understand why you thought it was me. It made sense. I was the only boy who showed any interest in Evie. Well, obviously, I wasn't the only boy. Do you know who it is?" When she shook her head, he snorted. "I don't get your sister. She should've told you the truth. Does the father even know?"

"Yes. I guess he's been sending money for Clint all along."

"He knows, but he hasn't come back to see his son? What a piece of shit."

She smiled as if he'd just said something wonderful, and in her eyes, he saw the same adoration he'd seen when she was thirteen. She moved closer, her foot brushing against his leg like a hot brand. He suddenly realized that without her sister in the way, there was nothing stopping him and Penny from getting together.

Nothing but his damn conscience.

He moved away from her. "You shouldn't be here. You shouldn't be swimming in your underwear with some guy who isn't boyfriend material. And I don't do relationships, Penny. I like being unattached with no responsibilities and I plan to stay that way. I'm only staying here until I can convince Lucas and Chester to quit being so stubborn and take the money Logan collected to rebuild their house. Then I'm headed to California. I know you think you want me, but you really don't. You want someone better. Someone who can commit."

She studied him for a long moment before she turned and swam to shore. It was for the best. He knew that. Too bad his body didn't agree. Desire slammed into him as he watched her climb out of the springs, her soaked panties clinging to the round curves of her butt like a second skin. He dove under and didn't resurface until he knew she'd be gone. Even then, he waited for a long time before he got out.

He should leave. Not just Mesquite Springs, but Texas. If anyone could talk Chester and Lucas into letting the town rebuild their house, it was Penny, not him. Cru should go back to the ranch, pack his things, and get the hell out of Dodge. It would be simpler for everyone.

He climbed up the bank and pushed through some scrub junipers growing by the springs. He had just reached for his shirt to dry off when a voice caused him to freeze.

"Knock-knock."

Like a shy, pubescent kid, he quickly covered himself with his shirt and turned around to see Penny sitting on a rock in just her underwear. "I thought you'd left," he said.

"Nope." She smiled at him and repeated herself. "Knock-knock."

He blew out his breath. "Who's there?"

"Whatcha."

"Whatcha who?"

"Whatcha so scared of, Cru Cassidy?"

It was a good question. One he didn't have an answer for. He turned away and dried off before he pulled on his jeans. When he had them zipped and buttoned, he turned back to her. "I just think you should know the truth. I'm not some misunderstood hero like Severus, Penny. I live for the moment and have no ties to anything or anyone—and I don't want any."

She shrugged. "Okay. I get it. You don't intend to stay here forever. I didn't think you would. When I said I wanted you last night, I didn't mean as my forever boyfriend. If I want a boyfriend, I could have one." He didn't doubt that for a second. Dylan or Boone would be more than happy to fill the slot. "But I don't want a boyfriend. I have to deal with my stubborn father and enough stubborn cowboys all day. I don't need to add another man to the mix. When I said I wanted you, what I meant was I wanted to . . . well, use you for sex."

He stared at her. "Excuse me?"

She laughed. "Don't look so surprised, Cru. Women can use men for sex just like men use women. But I can see how sex with me would frighten you. You think because I had a crush on you if you take me to bed, I'll fall madly in love with you." She shrugged as she hopped off the rock, her breasts bouncing enticingly in her wet bra. "And if that's how you see it, there's nothing I can do to convince you otherwise."

She placed a hand on her hip as if she wasn't wearing see-though underwear that made Cru's mouth dry. Then she gave him back the same words he'd spoken to her when she'd first invited him to the Gardener Ranch. "But I'm not going to hide from you, Cru. If I tempt you beyond your resistance, that's your problem, not mine."

# CHAPTER SIXTEEN

SEVERUS TUGGED AGAINST THE REINS and fidgeted sideways, eager for a much faster pace. But Penny held him in check. The horse might want to run, but she was quite content right where she was.

Sometimes life was as close to perfect as it could get. This was one of those times. Spring showers had arrived the first week of May and the range was now covered with wildflowers and sprouts of green grass. A cool breeze chilled the morning air, and the sun had just peeked its head up, painting the horizon in pretty pinks and purples. For as far as the eye could see, there was only vast cattle land. But it wasn't the May morning that made Penny feel so jubilant as much as the other things that were happening in her life.

Chester had gone ahead with the cataract surgery and could see much better. Lucas had gotten the doctor's okay to take off the boot and was walking fine. He also wasn't forgetting as many things as he had been now that he was no longer mixing medications. The doctor seemed to think depression and lack of purpose had also contributed to his memory loss. Working on the ranch had taken care of both, and Penny had no plans to fire the two cowboys even after they got their new house built.

The Double Diamond boys had collected enough money to rebuild Chester and Lucas's house. Now all they had to do was convince the two stubborn men to accept the money and let the town start planning a house-raising party.

Besides Chester and Lucas's good news, Evie was dropping off Clint at the beginning of June. Since Penny didn't want to change her sister's decision, she had decided not to hassle her about who Clint's father was until after the summer. If Clint's father didn't want to know his son, it was best to wait until Clint was a little older and more mature before springing the news on him. She didn't want her nephew to rebel any more than he already was.

And then there was Cru.

She glanced over at the cowboy riding next to her. When he'd first gotten there, his straw cowboy hat had been clean and new. Now it was sweat-stained and smudged with the red-clay dirt, the front brim bent to shade his flawless features and the pretty green of his eyes. The stripe in his plaid western shirt matched his eyes. He wore it like he wore all his other western shirts: open at the throat and cuffed at the sleeves to reveal his tanned, muscled forearms and strong hands that were draped over the saddle horn. He sat the horse like he belonged there. With just a flex of muscled thighs, he guided his mount away from Severus's fidgeting.

"That horse needs to be gelded," he said. "He's a little too full of himself."

She pulled her gaze away from Cru and concentrated on getting Severus under control. "Aren't most males? And you wouldn't like it very much if someone cut off your testicles. Besides, you're just mad because he tossed you on your butt the other day."

"And I don't want him doing the same to you."

"He's not going to throw me."

"Are you saying you're a better rider than I am?"

She flashed him a grin. "Yep."

He stared at her for only a second before he conceded. "Okay, so you're a better rider. But I still remember a time when you got tossed on your ass by a horse and I had to come to your rescue."

"I wish you hadn't. I was embarrassed as heck that you witnessed the entire thing."

He grinned. "And here I thought you were just flushed because you were sitting across my lap."

"That too."

He laughed. He had laughed often in the last couple weeks. Of course, so had she. Once she'd informed him that she just wanted him for sex, things had changed between them. Cru had relaxed around her and they'd formed a comfortable friendship that brightened Penny's days more than the sun peeking over the horizon. Not to say that she didn't have the occasional kiss flashback when he smiled at her in a certain way—like now. But she'd learned to ignore those desires and just enjoy the time they had left together.

Time that seemed to be sifting away too quickly.

"Did you see the news last night?" she asked. "There's another fire in California. They certainly have a lot of those. Not to mention earthquakes and mud slides."

"Would you quit trying to talk me out of going to California? Every place has its problems. Texas has bugs, humidity, and sassy cowgirls." He shot her a pointed look.

"I'm not sassy. That's Evie."

"I don't remember Evie being near as sassy as you."

"I'm only sassy to arrogant cowboys."

"This coming from the same woman who thinks she's the best rider in the state."

"That's not arrogance. That's just a fact." She sent him a cocky smile, but it soon faded. "You won't be happy in California. You love working a ranch and don't try to deny it. I know a true cowboy when I see one."

He glanced around and nodded. "I do enjoy being on a working ranch. I'd forgotten how much until now."

"You could always buy your own place," she continued. "My granddaddy used to say all anyone needs to be happy is a little piece of Texas and a dream."

He glanced over at her and grinned. "You should've been a lawyer or a car salesman with that persuasive tongue. But this drifter has no desire to settle down. Now, Miss Hot Shot Horsewoman, you need to put your money where your mouth is. If you beat me to the south fence, I'll buy you a double decker mint chocolate chip ice cream cone at the pharmacy. If I beat you, you treat me to a caramel chocolate swirl double decker."

"You're on." Without waiting for him to give the signal, she put her heels to Severus and took off. She gave the horse free rein, leaning her head close to his neck and coaxing him on. "Come on, boy. If we lose, I'll never hear the end of it."

They didn't lose. They arrived at the fence well before Cru. Although she had cheated a little. Something Cru immediately pointed out.

"You cheater!"

"I didn't cheat. You shouldn't ask someone if they want to race unless you're ready to go." She glanced at his bare head. "And you lost your hat, cowboy."

"I couldn't worry about my hat when I had to catch a cheat."

"Fine. You only have to buy me a single scoop of mint chocolate—" She cut off when she saw a white sedan parked on the other side of the fence. "What's that car doing parked in Chester and Lucas's north pasture?"

Cru followed her gaze and his eyes narrowed. "I don't know, but I'm going to find out." He dismounted and she followed suit. Holding onto the wooden fence post, he placed a boot on the second strand of barbwire, then used the post to vault over.

"You need help?" he asked when he was on the other side. "Or do you think you climb fences as well as you ride?"

"Smart butt." Since she was shorter, she had to climb the wire like a ladder and swing a leg over. Of course, the inside seam of her jeans snagged on a barb and Cru had to come to her rescue unless she wanted to rip a hole in them and her skin. His hand slid up the inside of her thigh and unhooked the denim. Before she could even suck in a breath at the tingle of heat that zinged straight to her panties, he easily lifted her over the fence.

"Did it cut you?" he asked once she was standing on solid ground. Except with his hands encircling her waist, she didn't feel like she was standing on solid ground. She felt unstable and wobbly. She lifted her gaze. His lips were parted and his breath whooshed in and out like he was having a hard time breathing. She was struggling to breathe too. Her hands tightened on his shoulders and his tightened on her waist. His head tipped and so did hers. Their lips moved toward each other in slow motion. But just as her eyes slid closed, a woman's voice had them flashing back open.

"You're the man who likes turnip greens."

She opened her eyes and turned her head to the woman walking toward them. Or carefully making her way toward them. High heels weren't exactly the best shoes to wear out on the range. To keep her pointy heels from sinking into the dirt, she was tiptoeing around the clumps of prairie grass. She still ended up stumbling. Cru released Penny and quickly moved to steady her before she took a header.

"Careful there, Devlin."

*Devlin*? Cru knew her?

Penny's gaze narrowed on the woman's hands as they settled on Cru's shoulders. Exactly where Penny's had been only moments before. She had wanted to punch guys before, but never a woman . . . until now.

"Thank you," Devlin said. "I'm such a klutz."

"You probably wouldn't be if you had on sensible shoes," Penny said.

Cru shot her a surprised glance, but she didn't feel the least bit remorseful for her rudeness when his hands still held the woman's waist.

"You're right," Devlin stepped out of his arms and pushed up her glasses. "It was quite stupid of me to come out here dressed like this."

Now that she wasn't touching Cru, Penny shouldn't feel so annoyed. But it was hard not to be annoyed with a woman who was tall, slender, and beautiful. And whom Cru knew so well.

"What *are* you doing on Chester and Lucas's land, Devlin?" he asked.

Devlin's eyes widened behind the lens of her glasses. "Chester and Lucas's? I thought this land was owned by Hank Gardener."

"You're off by just a little." Cru pointed to the fence. "The other side is Gardener Ranch. This side is Double Diamond Ranch. Don't tell me you tried to use your GPS again."

*How well did they know each other?* And what was this woman doing here looking all wide-eyed and confused at Cru. Was she an old girlfriend who had followed him here?

"I used a map this time," she said. "But obviously not well. I thought I was on Gardener land." A knot formed above the frame of her glasses. "But if my calculations are right that fence shouldn't be there."

"Why would you be calculating anything on Gardener land?" Penny asked.

Instead of Devlin answering, Cru did. "She's looking for oil."

Both Devlin and Penny glanced at him in surprise, but Devlin spoke first. "How did you know? Did Mr. Gardener tell you why I was here?"

"Mr. Gardener?" Penny said. "My daddy knows you're out here?"

Devlin turned to her. "Hank Gardener is your father? Oh, I'm sorry. I didn't realize you were his daughter. Yes, your father knows I'm here. I've spoken to him numerous times on the phone and we finally met in person a few weeks ago." She held out her hand. "I'm Devlin McMillian from Reliable Energy Resources. But I would appreciate it if you didn't repeat that to anyone. I don't want other energy companies trying to profit from my research."

Penny wasn't concerned about another energy company finding out Devlin was here. She was concerned about the fact that her father had talked to Devlin and never said a word to her about it. Not one word. Of course, why would he? He had never valued her input. He only cared about what he wanted. And why was he allowing an energy company to do a survey when he'd always been against drilling or anything that tore up his land?

"So my father is completely receptive to the idea of drilling?" she asked.

Devlin looked confused. "Most people are happy about striking oil. You could stand to make a lot of money and your father seems to know that. And all my calculations say there's oil here. Or not here, but on your land."

"Yes, it is my land, Devlin—as much as my daddy likes to think otherwise. And until I talk with my father, I don't want you nosing around on it." She knew she was being rude, but she couldn't help it. She was furious with her father for not telling her about their meeting. And she became even madder when Cru stuck up for Devlin.

"Wait a minute, Penny," Cru said. "It's not Devlin's fault. She got permission from your father and is just doing her job."

"Well, she's not going to do her job here!" She whirled and headed back to the fence. When she got there, she stopped to see if Cru was coming. He wasn't. He was helping Devlin in her stupid high heels back to her car. Once they got there, he pulled out his cellphone like he was getting her number. Which really ticked Penny off. And she'd be damned if she'd wait for him to set up a date.

She climbed on the lower strand of barbwire and swung her leg over. Of course, her jeans got stuck on a barb again. But this time, she didn't care about ripping her pants. She swung her other leg over with a loud rip of denim that had both Devlin and Cru looking at her. She wanted to flip them off so badly she had to clench her hands into fists. She quickly untethered Severus and mounted. She intended to ride out her anger in a fast run, but the skittish stallion felt her agitation and refused to cooperate. He reared and would've tossed her off if she hadn't had a good seat. By the time she had him under control, Cru had climbed the fence.

"I told you that horse needs gelding."

She couldn't help taking some of her anger out on him. "So did you set up a date with Miss Stupid High Heels?"

He arched an eyebrow at her before he mounted his horse. "No, but I did get her number. I figured that once you cool down you'll want to apologize for your temper tantrum."

"Temper tantrum! I did not throw a temper tantrum." She reined Severus around and headed back the way she came. Since the stallion was still being ornery, Cru easily caught up.

"I don't know what you'd call it. And it looks like you're not over it. Go ahead. If you need to vent, vent."

He was right. She did need to vent. Even Severus sensed it.

"How could he do it?" she said. "How could my father talk about drilling on the ranch and not mention a word to me? Not only am I his daughter, I'm the ranch manager. Of course, he doesn't treat me like a manager. He treats me like his slave. The only time he talks to me is to issue an order. 'Do this, Penelope Anne. Do that.' Well, I'm sick and tired of it."

She glanced over at Cru, expecting him to be smirking at her rant. Instead, his gaze was serious.

"You should be sick and tired of it. And you need to tell your father that."

"What good will it do? It won't change anything."

"It will if you tell him you're going to leave the ranch if he doesn't start treating you as an equal partner in it."

She snorted. "Evie tried that and he told her to get the hell out. And I don't want to leave the ranch. I love it too much."

"I get it, Penny." He glanced around. "There's a lot to love. But you shouldn't let your fear of losing it make you a slave to your father's every whim."

"I'm not a slave to his every whim."

He raised his eyebrows. "That's not how I see it. You never go up against him on anything. Even when you're right and he's wrong. And you don't go up against your sister either. You should be mad at her for keeping the truth about Clint's father from you. Instead, you just accept your father's and sister's inconsiderate behavior and act like you're not hurt. But you are. I've seen it in your eyes after you talk to your sister or have an argument with your father. I've seen how hurt you are that they treat you like a kid instead of an equal."

The truth was never easy to accept, which was probably why she refused to. "I'm not hurt. That's just part of being the youngest in the family. No one takes you seriously."

"That might've been true when you were a little girl, but it shouldn't be true now that you're a grown woman."

"So what am I supposed to do? Disown them because they're too stubborn to listen to my views? That's not what you do when you love someone, Cru. When you love someone, you put up with their imperfections. But you wouldn't know that, would you? Because after what your mother did, you're too afraid to love anyone." As soon as the words were out, she wanted them back. She glanced over at him. "I'm sorry. I didn't mean that. I had no right to say—"

He cut her off. "You have every right. It's okay to argue with people, Penny. It's okay to stand up for yourself and say what's on your mind. Sometimes people need to be called out. Especially when it's the truth. I have no business telling you how to live your life when I've made a mess of mine. And you're right. I'm scared to death of getting attached to anything or anyone. Scared that they'll leave me just like my mom did. It's pretty damned silly when you think about it. But I guess the things that happen to us when we're young have a big impact on our adult lives. You watched your sister go against your father and get kicked off the ranch and you don't want the same thing to happen to you. But I don't think it will. Your father needs you more than you know. He would be stupid to let you go when you're the one who runs this place. The one who makes sure that everything is running smoothly and all the ranch hands are happy. If people had to deal with your father, you wouldn't be able to keep a ranch hand to save your—"

A low bellow cut him off.

They both turned to the cluster of mesquite to the right. Through the tangled branches, you could just see a pair of dark calf eyes.

"I'll get him." Cru unhooked his rope from his saddle horn and took off toward the bushes. Penny would usually be right there with him. But she was so stunned by his speech she just watched as he untangled the calf from the bushes and led him back to his horse by the rope.

Cru had gotten it all wrong. She didn't go up against her father because she was worried about getting kicked off the ranch. She didn't go up against him because she wanted her family reunited again. She wanted Evie and Clint here where they belonged, even if it meant she had to kiss her father's butt. Because, like Cru, she never wanted to feel the loss of losing someone she loved like she had felt the loss of losing her mom. Except her mother's death hadn't caused her to push loved ones away. It had caused her to pull them close and refuse to let go.

Even at the cost of her own principles.

She had always thought of herself as a tough cowgirl. And she *was* tough on the range. She could ride and rope and tackle a steer to the ground as well as any man. But with her family, she was still a little girl who couldn't stand up for herself or her beliefs. Her father, and even her sister, had taken advantage of that.

And it was time she stopped letting them.

# CHAPTER SEVENTEEN

CRU KNEW PENNY WAS UPSET. She didn't say a word on the ride to take the calf back to its herd. She didn't laugh when he found his hat and pulled it back on only to discover it was completely bent out of shape. She didn't even crack a smile at his knock-knock jokes. And he thought the mustache knock-knock joke was the funniest one he'd found on the Internet. By the time they reached the barn, he was feeling pretty bad for taking the smile off her face. He should've kept his big mouth shut. Instead, he'd given her a lecture. And the last thing Penny needed was another lecturing father.

"Did you find the calf?" Raul came out of the barn to get their horses with Trixie close on his heels. As soon as Penny dismounted, the dog hobbled over to greet her. Usually she crouched down and let the dog give her exuberant kisses. But today, she only gave Trixie a brief ear scratch before she spoke to Raul.

"Where's my father?"

"He's in the back paddock with that new horse he bought. But he's in a pretty bad mood, so I'd wait to talk to him."

"I'm in a bad mood too," she said as she headed for the corral. The purposeful way she strode around the barn made Cru realize things were about to get ugly. And it was all his fault. If Penny got kicked off her beloved ranch, he would never forgive himself.

He hurried to catch up with her. "You shouldn't listen to me, Penny. I've never had a family. So I don't have a clue what I'm talking about. You're right to respect your father. And you certainly don't want to go off half-cocked on him just because an idiot says you should stand up for yourself."

She didn't stop. "I'm not half-cocked. I'm fully-cocked. And you were right. It's about time I stopped acting like a little girl."

"That's all good, but maybe you should wait until you've cooled down."

"When I cool down, I'll make excuses for his behavior just like I always do." She opened the gate of the paddock and swung it wide. Hank Gardener was trying to put a saddle on the appaloosa horse. When the gate clanked against the barn, the horse startled and pranced away.

"Close the damned gate!" he yelled. "Don't you have a brain in your head, Penelope Anne?"

Okay, so maybe Hank did deserve a good ass chewing. And Cru was sticking around to see it . . . and to make sure Penny didn't get too crazy. Although she already looked pretty crazed. And sexy as hell.

She strode into the paddock like a princess warrior and slammed the gate closed, causing Cru to jump back out of the way or get hit. Figuring it was safer to be on this side of the fence anyway, he rested his arms on the gate and watched Penny stride toward her father. She jerked off her hat and the sun reflected off her fiery hair like a brand new penny. And she was sure acting like one. She stopped within inches of her father and got right in his face.

"Yes, I have a brain in my head, Daddy. Even though you don't think I do. Why didn't you tell me an energy company had contacted you about drilling for oil on our land?"

Hank Gardener didn't even flinch. Of course, Cru didn't expect him to. From what he could tell, the man was made of stone.

"Because it was none of your business."

Cru waited for Penny to explode. He sure would have. But she only stared at her father for a long minute before she released her breath. "Of course you think that. You've always thought that. The only one who needs to know about ranch business is you. Your wife didn't need to know anything. Evie doesn't need to know anything. And I sure as hell don't need to know anything. But you're wrong, Daddy. You're dead wrong. This ranch is my business. And it's Evie's. And it was Mama's. We've all worked hard to make this ranch what it is."

Hank leaned closer. "You don't know what you're talking about, little girl. I'm the one who paid for this ranch in full with my blood, sweat, and tears."

Penny didn't back down. "And you think I haven't given this ranch my blood, sweat, and tears? I work my ass—"

"Watch your mouth! I won't have a daughter of mine talking like a saddle tramp."

"But it's okay for you to. That's bullshit, Daddy."

Cru couldn't help but grin. That grin faded when Hank jerked off his hat and his face was bright red with anger. Cru stepped up onto the corral railing. If Hank lifted one finger to Penny, Cru was going to kick his ass from here to Simple. But Hank didn't lift a finger. He just stood there shaking with anger while Penny continued to gore the bull.

"In case you haven't noticed, Daddy. I'm not a little girl anymore. I'm a grown woman."

Hank might not have noticed, but Cru definitely had. For the last few weeks, he'd tried to act like he could resist her, but his gaze kept being drawn to those womanly curves and his mind kept going back to the kisses they'd shared. Kisses that were permanently embossed on his brain. And no amount of knock-knock jokes or friendly conversation could get them out. It was a struggle every time he was with her not to drag her into his arms for a repeat. And right now, with her hair all wild and her face flushed with temper, it was an even bigger struggle.

"And as a grown woman," she continued. "I'll damned well cuss if I want to."

"Like hell you will! This is my ranch and my house and I set the rules!"

"Haven't you been listening to a word I've been saying? This isn't—"

Sadie moved up next to Cru and pulled his attention away from Penny. "What in the world is going on? I can hear Hank yelling all the way in the house."

"Penny and Hank are going at it."

"Well, I'm not about to let my sweet little chick be browbeaten by that stubborn cuss." She started to open the gate, but Cru stopped her.

"Give her a minute. I think your little chick has turned into an angry goose." Cru returned his attention to the paddock where Penny was now standing on the toes of her boots, pointing a finger at her father.

". . . and you need to get it through your thick skull that this ranch is as much mine and Evie's as it is yours!"

"Your sister doesn't give a hoot about this ranch."

"Yes, she does, Daddy. She loves this ranch as much as I do. She just couldn't stay here and be under your thumb. She couldn't stay here and be her own woman." She froze with her finger in his face. Suddenly, all the temper seemed to drain out of her and she lowered down to her boot heels. When she spoke, she spoke more to herself than her father. "And I can't stay here either. I can't stay here if I want to be my own woman. No matter how much I want my family reunited, I can't stay."

Holy shit. This was not what Cru had intended

to happen. He had only wanted Penny to threaten to leave the ranch to make Hank back down. He never thought that she'd actually do it. She loved this ranch. She'd be miserable anywhere else.

But that was exactly what was happening. Without another word to her father, she tugged on her hat and strode toward the gate. He planned to hold the gate closed and talk her out of this nonsense, but Sadie pushed him out of the way and opened it for her.

"I'll help you pack, honey."

"No!" He followed them toward the house. "You can't pack your bags. You can't leave. Just give your father some time and I'm sure he'll come to his senses."

"No, he won't. The damned stubborn fool will never come to his senses. And I'm tired of trying." Penny stomped up the steps of the porch. "I'm going to go stay with Evie. She had the right idea all along." She jerked open the screen door and strode inside.

Cru held it for Sadie and followed behind the two women. "You can't go to Abilene, Penny. It's not the place for you."

She hesitated and turned to him. "You're right. I can't be my own woman in my sister's house where I'll still be her kid sister." She thought for a moment. "I guess I'll have to move somewhere else. Maybe Dallas." She headed down a hallway.

He followed trying to think of anything that would change her mind. He didn't have a home, but she did. And he wasn't going to be the reason she lost it. "Dallas is an awful choice for you. Tons of people, crime, and traffic. A small town girl like you will hate it there."

Penny paused outside a bedroom. One quick peek inside and he knew whose room it was. There was no pink or ruffles or frills. The furnishings were sturdy and simple. Pictures of horses hung on all the walls and plain white curtains fluttered in the breeze sweeping in through the open window. The oak bed was unmade, the white comforter and yellow sheets mussed and the pillows scattered like someone had been making wild love in it.

"You're right. Why should I leave my hometown?" Penny's question pulled Cru away from ogling her bed and thinking about things he had no business thinking about. "I can't stay on the ranch, but that doesn't mean I have to leave Simple. I could even get a job on one of the other ranches. And if Daddy doesn't like it, he can just go to hell." She walked into her room and slammed the door behind her.

Cru lifted his hand to knock, but Sadie stopped him. "Best to give her a moment. She's in quite a lather. And I'd say it's about time."

"It's my fault. I'm the one who got her riled up about standing up to her father. But I didn't think she'd actually leave the ranch. She'll be miserable. She loves this ranch. It's her home. And I couldn't live with myself if I'm responsible for taking her away from it."

Sadie studied him. "And here I thought you were just trying to get in her pants like you were Evie's."

Cru stared at her in surprise, and she laughed. "You and Penny certainly thought no one had eyes in their heads back then, didn't you?" She waved a hand. "Come on into the kitchen while I call Evie to let her know what happened."

He glanced back at the bedroom door. "But I need to stop her from making the worst mistake of her life."

"Good luck with that. Once a Gardener makes up their mind, there's no changing it. Stubbornness runs in the family. Besides, it's way past time for her to leave and spread her wings. It will be good for her. And hopefully knock some sense into her father."

"But what if it doesn't? What if Hank never says he's sorry and never gets her to come back?"

"He'll do it or he'll be gettin' worms with his oatmeal."

Cru wasn't so sure that worms would make a difference to Hank, but maybe going a few days without his ranch manager would. He followed Sadie to the kitchen and sat at the table while she talked to Evie. From what he could get from the conversation, Evie was thrilled her sister had told off their father and ticked at Hank for forcing Penny to leave the home she loved.

Although Penny didn't look like anyone was forcing her when she walked into the kitchen pulling a roller suitcase behind her. She looked determined and still mad as a wet hen. "I'm staying at Dixon's Boardinghouse. Reba said I could have the garden room."

"That's the prettiest room in the place." Sadie gave Penny a big hug. Cru could see tears in both the women's eyes and it made him feel even worse. Sadie smoothed Penny's hair. "I want you to think of this as a much-needed vacation. Don't you worry about the ranch. With Dylan, Chester, Lucas, and Cru's help, I'll keep everything running smoothly until you get back."

Cru didn't want to keep the ranch running smoothly without Penny. At that moment, he realized how much he'd loved working with her these past weeks. How happy he'd felt every morning when he woke up knowing that she'd be waiting in the barn for him. When he followed her outside, he couldn't help taking the suitcase away from her.

"Would you just listen to me for a second?"

"I did listen to you and you're absolutely right. I've been acting like a little girl and expecting to be treated like a woman."

"No, you weren't. You were acting like a loving daughter." Leaving the suitcase on the porch, he led her down the steps and toward the barn. Raul wasn't around, but he still pulled Penny into an empty stall for privacy. "When I told you to stand up to your father, I didn't mean for you to actually leave. I only meant for you to threaten to leave."

"Threats don't work with my daddy. Only actions." She kicked at the pile of hay with her boot. "Stubborn ass."

"You can't leave, Penny. You won't be happy any place but here." The tears that filled her eyes were all the proof he needed. "Dammit." He ran a hand through his hair. "What have I done?" He turned back to her. "Look, I'll talk to your dad. I'll tell him that you didn't mean anything you said."

"I meant everything I said. I love this ranch, but I'm tired of being a compliant daughter who never speaks up for her beliefs. I'm tired of working my butt off and not getting a say in what happens to this ranch. I'm tired of being treated like a little girl who doesn't have a brain and doesn't know what she wants." She studied him. "And if I want to start being treated like a woman who knows what she wants, I better start acting like it."

Before he knew what was happening, she grabbed the front of his shirt and backed him up against the wall of the stall.

"What are you—" That was all he got out before her lips touched his. Or not touched as much as devoured. She took what she wanted with demanding lips and a ravenous tongue. He was toast. Complete and total toast as desire set him ablaze like a range fire. As her mouth controlled the heat sizzling through him, her hands tightened on his shirt and tugged open the snaps. His abdominal muscles jumped in response as her cool fingers spread over them, then slowly trailed a scorching path up to his pecs.

She cupped them firmly in her hands before she pulled away from his lips and trailed kisses over his chin, down his throat, across one collarbone to his left nipple. The wet heat of her mouth had his head thumping back against the stall wall and a groan escaping his throat as desire settled hard and thick beneath the fly of his jeans. He had never wanted to bury himself deep inside a woman so much in his life. He wanted to lose himself in her and never be found. It was the intensity of his need that had him pushing her away.

They were both breathing heavily. And when she opened her eyes, he could see the dazed passion that tightened her pupils into tiny points. He felt just as dazed. But he couldn't give her what she needed. Even if he desperately wanted to.

"I'm sorry, Penny. But as much as I want to have sex with you, that's all it would be. Sex. And you deserve more. Much more."

He expected her to turn tail and run. That's what the Penny of a few days ago would've done. But this Penny wasn't scared off so easily. Her eyes narrowed with determination.

"Don't tell me what I deserve, Cru Cassidy. I'm not that thirteen-year-old crushing girl you first met. I'm a woman who can handle a sexual relationship without needing a ring and wedding bells." She grabbed his shirt and pulled him in for another kiss before she pushed him away. "I'll be staying at Dixon's Boardinghouse."

She turned on a boot heel and strutted out of the stall, leaving Cru stunned and desperately wanting something he couldn't have.

# CHAPTER EIGHTEEN

"**B**UT WHY WOULD YOU GO to Dixon's when you could've come here? I'm your sister!"

Penny put her cellphone on speaker so her eardrum wouldn't be busted by Evie's yelling and set it on the nightstand next to the vase of lilacs. The garden room at Dixon's Boardinghouse was decorated like a quaint country cottage. While it was beautiful, it was a little too girly for Penny's taste. She missed her bedroom with the hickory furniture Grandpa Myers had made for her mama when she was a child and all the pictures of the beloved horses she'd owned over the years.

Including Severus. She missed the feisty horse. She missed him as much as she missed the ranch and Sadie, Raul, Trixie, Dylan, and all the ranch hands. She even missed her daddy. Darn his stubborn hide.

She pushed down her melancholy and reminded herself it was time to put on her big girl panties and quit acting like a homesick kid at summer camp. "You don't need your little sister living with you."

"And yet, you wanted me to come back to the ranch and live with you."

Evie *did* have a good point. "Okay, so maybe I've finally grown up and realized that adults need to have their own lives."

"You could have your own life living with me. I'm not going to try to bulldoze you like Daddy."

"No, you'll just mother me to death like you do Clint. Besides, what if you get married? You can't expect me to live with newlyweds. That's just weird, Evie."

"What's weird is you living at Dixon's Boardinghouse where you don't even have your own bathroom. You have to share with strangers."

That was going to take some getting used to. While the garden room was cozy and quaint with its four-poster bed, overstuffed floral reading chair, and French doors leading out to Reba's beautiful garden, it would be nice to have her own on suite bathroom.

"You have a point. This morning, I ran into Miss Gertie coming out of the bathroom in her wrinkled birthday suit. She just rolled right past me with her cat Rhett Butler sitting in the plastic basket of her walker as if she wasn't naked as a jaybird. But I wouldn't have my own bathroom at your house either," she said. "I'd have to share with Clint. And I love my nephew to death, but he's a little piggy."

"Tell me about it. He cleans his room and within an hour it smells like a boys' locker room again."

"Sadie will whip him into shape when he gets to the ranch."

"What are you talking about? I'm not sending him to the ranch this summer if you're not there to watch out for him."

Penny had been afraid of that. "You can't do that to him, Evie. Clint is so excited about coming to the ranch this summer. And so is Daddy. Just because I'm mad at Dad doesn't mean you have to be mad at him too."

"I never stopped being mad at him. He's a jerk. And I'm so proud of you for giving him hell for once. He more than deserved it."

Penny couldn't argue the point. But she couldn't help feeling bad for him either. When Evie left, he still had her. Now both his daughters were gone. As ticked as she was at him, she didn't want him to lose his grandson too. "Please think about letting Clint stay on the ranch this summer. Maybe being around Clint will soften him up a little and make him see the error of his ways."

Evie snorted. "If you're expecting an apology, I wouldn't hold my breath. He probably doesn't even think that going behind your back with the energy company was a big deal."

"You're right. He said it was none of my business." Penny plumped up one of the fluffy pillows on the bed with her fist. The pillowcase was a crisp white cotton with pretty embroidered lilacs around the edge. The other pillows on the bed were embroidered with different flowers—roses, daisies, and impatiens. No doubt, Reba's grandmother, Miss

Gertie, had done the delicate handwork. The old woman was meaner than sin, but could certainly stitch a fine seam.

"I thought Daddy was against drilling," Evie said. "He used to fume and fuss every time we drove by a new pump jack."

"I did too." Penny leaned back on the pillow and tucked her feet up on the bed. "You should've seen him cuss out the guy who stopped by to see if his company could lease some land for wind turbines. Which is why letting some energy company lease our land to survey for oil just doesn't make sense."

"Maybe he needs the money."

"I don't know why he would. Cattle prices are up and the ranch should be doing great. Not that I'd know since he insists on doing all the book-keeping himself."

"So what are you going to do now?"

It was a good question. "I don't have a clue. I guess I need to get a job."

"Doing what? The only thing you'll be happy doing is ranching."

"Then I'll get a job with one of the other ranches."

"You know that will make Daddy have a con-niption fit."

"Yep."

Evie laughed. "You have grown some balls, baby sister."

"Not really. I'm scared to death to be on my own. But sometimes a girl has to do what a girl has to do." An image of Cru flashed into her head. She should be embarrassed by how she attacked him in the barn, but she wasn't. She'd wanted Cru for what felt like forever. It was time she owned up to it. Even with her sister.

"I like Cru."

There was a long stretch of silence before Evie heaved a sigh. "I was afraid of that. I hoped you'd grown out of your crush, but when I saw you two together at the hospital, I knew you hadn't."

"You knew I had a crush on Cru?"

"Everyone knew you had a crush on Cru. It was pretty obvious, Pen."

"And yet, you let me believe he was Clint's father and confront him about it."

"You confronted Cru about being Clint's father? Why would you do that?"

"Because I really believed it was him. You liked each other that summer. And I saw you kiss him."

"Yeah, I liked him like a little brother. And he kissed me. I didn't kiss him. If you'd spied longer, you would've seen me push him away. Not only because I wasn't interested in kissing Cru, but also because my little sister liked him. And I would never break the sister rule."

Penny leaned her head back and stared up at the ceiling. "Well, I broke it. I thought you and Cru had gotten together and I kissed him anyway. Twice."

"Why, you slut."

She sat up. "Evie!"

Evie laughed. "I'm kidding. Geez, Pen, you're so serious sometimes. You didn't break any rules because Cru is not the one I got with that summer. And I should've told you it wasn't him. Especially after I saw the way you two were looking at each other in the hospital. I guess I was hoping that if you thought he was Clint's father, you'd stay away from him. You're still my baby sister and I want to protect you."

"I'm a big girl, Evie. I can take care of myself. But my relationship with Cru isn't going anywhere. All we shared were a few kisses and some knock-knock jokes."

It was a lie. They had shared much more than that. While working the ranch together, they had become friends. He had told her about living at St. James's Children Home and she had told him about her childhood on the ranch. He had shared stories about Father Stephen and the nuns and she had shared stories about her family.

A family she still couldn't help trying to keep together.

"Please let Clint come out for the summer," she said. "Please give him the opportunity to love the ranch as much as I do . . . as much as you do. Daddy isn't as grumpy with him as he is with us. And it's not like there won't be a lot of people there to keep an eye on him. You know Sadie will protect him with her life. And I'll be around if he has any problems or just needs to talk."

Evie released her breath. "Fine. I'll let him come. Clint would kill me if I changed my mind anyway. He's been packed for the last week. And maybe I'll stay a couple days and hang out with my little sister and visit with Chester and Lucas."

"I'd love that and so will they. Although they won't have much time for visiting. They'll be getting ready to move into their new house."

"How did you get them to go along with the house raising?"

"We didn't. Sadie and I decided that it's best if we just build it and let them raise holy hell afterwards." A knock on the door startled Penny. "Listen, Evie, someone's at the door, I have to go."

"I'm not going until you find out who it is."

Penny rolled her eyes as she got to her feet. "City life has made you a scaredy cat. It's probably Reba with a plate of snickerdoodle cookies. She promised she'd bring some up when they came out of the oven. I'll call you later." She hung up the phone and hurried to the door.

But it wasn't Reba holding a plate of snicker-doodles. It was Cru. He was hatless and it looked like he'd been running his fingers through his hair because the raven locks were mussed and sexier than usual. He looked tired, his eyes red-rimmed like he hadn't gotten a lot of sleep the night before. But the rest of him looked spit-polished, from his starched western shirt to his pressed jeans and polished boots. She felt like a complete slob in her stretched out t-shirt and comfy gray sweatpants with her hair up in a messy bun on the top of her head.

"What are you doing here?" she asked. "Did something happen at the ranch?"

He lifted the plate. "Reba asked me to bring

these to you."

"You came here to bring me snickerdoodles?"

His cheeks turned pink. She'd never seen Cru blush before . . . or act so awkward. He shuffled his boots and cleared his throat. "So did you mean what you said in the barn?"

"About not coming back to the ranch?"

"No. About—" He held out the plate. "Could you put these somewhere? I can't talk with a plate of snicker-whatevers in my hands."

She took the cookies and carried them to the little glass table by the French doors. When she turned, Cru was standing right behind her. His gaze was intense as he studied her.

"I like your hair like that."

She fiddled with the strangling strands. "It's a mess."

"It's beautiful. It's always beautiful." He lifted his hand as if to touch it, but then tightened it into a fist and let it drop. "Look, I came here because I just want to make sure that you understand."

"At this point, I don't understand anything. If you could just be a little more specific—"

Her words cut off when he pulled her to him and kissed her. Not a little peck, but a deep, greedy kiss that turned her mind to mush and her bones to butter. When he drew away, she had to hang onto his shoulders to keep from slipping to the floor.

"I want you, Penelope Anne Gardener," he said. "I've wanted you ever since I almost ran over you with my Porsche. And that want has grown into something I just don't understand. It's not the kind of want like when I want a burger because I'm hungry or a pillow because I'm tired. This is a deep, aching need that has almost been the death of me these past few weeks."

She knew exactly what he was talking about. The ache in her was almost unbearable. And it made her feel even more melty that he felt the same way.

"You ache for me?"

He smoothed a strand of her hair back from her face and his hand trembled as if he was trying hard to keep a handle on his emotions. "Like I've never ached for any woman in my life. And I want to ease that ache. I want to spend the entire night easing that ache deep inside of you." If a woman could reach orgasm just by words, Penny was on the brink. "But I need to know you understand that a night of sex is all I can offer."

If it were any other man asking for a one-night stand, she'd tell him to get the hell out. But this was Cru, and she understood he was giving her all he thought he could give. All he knew how to give. And she was willing to take whatever he offered.

She took his hand and held it to her lips, pressing a kiss to the callus in the center of his palm. "I understand."

His fingers curled around her chin and he lifted it until their gazes locked. "Promise me you won't get hurt."

She spoke just about a whisper. "I promise."

His breath whooshed out as if he'd been holding it, then he lowered his head and kissed her. This kiss wasn't as desperate as the previous one. This kiss was slow and thorough and as perfect as a kiss could get. When he finally pulled back, Penny felt lightheaded and woozy. She kept her eyes closed and wrapped her arms around his waist for balance, letting her head rest against his hard chest. Beneath her ear, she could hear the rapid thump of his heart.

"Your heart is beating fast," she said.

"You seem to have that effect on it." His fingers gently furrowed into her bun and pulled the hair tie free, allowing her hair to fall around her face and shoulders. Cru gathered the wild mass into his hands and tugged until she lifted her head for another kiss. Time seemed to stand still as they stood there exploring each other's mouths with insatiable lips and marauding tongues. And she wanted time to stand still. She wanted this moment to last forever.

Finally, he drew back and swept her t-shirt over her head. She wasn't wearing a bra. When he glanced down at her bare breasts, he made a sound deep in the back of his throat that was part growl and part groan. He stared at her breasts for so long she should've felt uncomfortable. She didn't. Right now, she was Cru's to do with what he wanted. And he was hers.

She slid her fingers inside the open neck of his shirt and tugged each snap open one at a time. When she reached the end, she pressed her open palms to his lower abdomen like she had done in the barn, then slowly slid her hands up each hard ridge and tempting hollow until she reached his collarbone. She pushed the shirt off his shoulders and studied the sculptured body before her like he still studied her.

"You're perfect," she said.

"Not even close," he answered before he hooked the waistband of her sweatpants with his fingers and pushed them down her hips. Once she was standing completely naked in the pool of cotton, he spoke in a croaked whisper. "Now you, on the other hand, are the definition of perfect."

He gave her one more sizzling onceover before he scooped her up in his arms and carried her to the bed. He laid her across it, her legs dangling over the edge. But before she could scoot up, he knelt on the floor in front of her and parted her legs. While she could deal with him looking at her boobs, she couldn't deal with him looking at her there. She tried to close her legs, but he held them open.

"I want to see you," he said. She sucked in her breath as his warm lips settled on the inside of her left knee. "I want to taste you."

Her breath remained lodged in her chest as he kissed his way up her thigh, his mouth and tongue leaving a trail of moist heat. She thought she'd felt like melted butter before. When his mouth finally settled on her quivering center, she felt like some-one had lit a match to the melted butter and set her aflame.

She gasped and her legs reflexively tightened against his head. But this time, instead of want-

ing to hold him out, she wanted to hold him in.
She wanted him to never stop the gentle kisses, the
deep pulls, and the sizzling flicks. He fanned the
fire higher and higher inside her until it exploded
in a shower of intense sensation that left her paw-
ing at his back with her bare feet and rambling in
a jumble of incoherent words.

"Oh . . . please . . . damn . . . so good . . . I . . . yes!"

After the sparks settled inside her and she was
left with only glowing embers, she puddled into
the mattress like a boneless mass of contentment
and smiled at the ceiling fan that whirled overhead.

"Wow."

She could feel Cru's breathy chuckle. He gave
her one last sweet kiss that sent an aftershock rip-
pling through her before he removed her limp legs
from his shoulders and got to his feet. He sat on
the edge of the bed to remove his boots and socks,
then stood back up to peel off his jeans and briefs.
She knew she had thoroughly enjoyed the oral sex,
and from the looks of things, so had he.

"You're a little bigger than when I spied on you
out at Mesquite Springs when you were fifteen,"
she said teasingly.

"That was called shrinkage. Something I haven't
had to deal with since I saw how you had grown
up." He pulled his wallet from his jeans and set it
on the nightstand before he leaned a knee on the
bed. "Now scoot over so we can continue doing
naughty grown up things."

She scooted over and he lay down next to her.
When she'd been thirteen, she'd fantasized about

kissing him. Since he'd come back, she'd fantasized about this—about lying naked with him and doing whatever she wanted with his hot body. But now that it was a reality, she felt a little overwhelmed. Cru seemed to sense her trepidation and he didn't push her. He lay on his side next to her and smoothed her hair back with gentle fingers as he gazed into her eyes. The emotion she read in those spring-green eyes said she wasn't just a one-night stand to him. She was more. Not enough to hold him forever, but enough to make her realize she didn't want to waste one second of their time together because she was nervous.

She pushed him over to his back and straddled him.

His eyebrows lifted. "So that's how it's gonna be, Miss Gardener?"

She smiled. "That's how it's gonna be, Mr. Cassidy."

He held open his arms. "Do with me what you will, cowgirl."

She did.

Taking her time, she explored every inch of his hot skin and hard muscles. First with her hands and then with her mouth. And he let her, not saying a word, just releasing deep "mmms" when she hit the spots he liked the most. Although she didn't need to hear his moans of desire to know how her touches affected him. His fists clenched and his legs grew restless as she moved closer and closer to his rigid length. When she finally took him in hand, his control snapped and he rolled her over and slid deep inside her.

She had been a little worried about the fit. But he fit just right. Perfect, in fact. For a moment, she felt sad that once he left, she would never feel so right again. But then he started to thrust and she forgot about the clock ticking off time. Soon all she could think about was holding on to this moment and this man for as long as he'd let her.

# CHAPTER NINETEEN

"DID YOU KNOW YOU HAVE a little mole right here? No, wait. I think that's a snickerdoodle crumb." Cru nibbled on Penny's stomach. He didn't realize he'd hit a ticklish spot until she squirmed and giggled. "Yep, a cookie crumb," he said against her soft skin. "But let me get another nibble just to be sure."

"Stop, Cru," she gasped in between laughter. But he liked hearing her laughter too much to stop. She finally used her feet to push him away and shoved him right off the end of the bed. "Oh my gosh!" Her concerned blue eyes peeked over the edge of the mattress at him. Eyes that he was going to have one hell of a time forgetting. And maybe he didn't want to forget them. As painful as it was going to be, he wanted to remember every second of the time he spent with Penny.

And he wasn't finished making those memories yet.

He got to his knees and slid his hand through her messy bedhead hair and kissed her. He would never grow tired of kissing these lips. Even if he kissed them a million times before he left. He was certainly working on that million. He greedily feasted on her luscious mouth before his stomach grumbled and he drew away.

"Miss Reba needs to get bigger beds. And room service. Man can't live on snickerdoodles alone."

"Reba doesn't serve lunch. She only serves breakfast and supper. And only at specific times." She glanced at the clock on the nightstand. "When do you have to get back to the ranch?"

It was so like Penny to always be thinking of the ranch. It reinforced his belief that she'd never be happy away from her home. "I'm playing hooky all day," he said with another kiss. "Just don't tell the boss." He meant it as a joke, but he should've known it was too soon for teasing.

A scowl wrinkled her forehead. "You don't have to worry about that. I don't have anything to say to my daddy."

He got to his feet. "Yes, you do. You have plenty to say to him. But after talking with Sadie, I agree that you leaving for a few days is for the best. It will give you time to cool down and him time to wise up."

"He's never going to wise up. Which is why I can never go back?" She flopped against the pillows. It was hard to keep his mind on their conversation with all her gorgeous flesh on display. But the hurt in her eyes overshadowed his lust.

He lay down next to her and pulled her into his arms, resting his chin on her head. "You'll go back.

You'll go back because it's where you belong. It's your home."

"It was a home when my mama and Evie were living there. Now it's just a place I fight with my daddy."

"That's not true and you know it. You might not get along with your father all the time, but you love him and he loves you. You can see it in his eyes every time he looks at you. He's just too stubborn to outwardly show it. Some people are just like that."

She lifted her head. "Like you."

He stared into her clear blue eyes and realized he cared for this woman. Cared for her deeply. Words to express that caring pushed at the back of his throat, wanting release. All he had to do was open his mouth and he knew they'd easily pop out. But it wasn't saying the words that counted. It was proving them. Love wasn't just words. It was actions. It was making a commitment to be there for someone no matter what. It wasn't telling them you loved them one second and leaving them in a bathroom stall the next.

And he had the same genes as his mother. He'd proven his lack of commitment time and time again with jobs, apartment leases, and women. As much as he thought he wanted to commit to Penny, he was terrified that in a month or two his feelings would change and he'd want to leave.

Which was why he didn't release the words. Instead, he kissed her and distracted her from their conversation by gliding his hands over her tempting body and caressing all the places he'd discovered made her moan. When she was senseless with need, he made slow, tender, love to her. Communicating with his body what he would never communicate with words.

Sapped of mental and physical strength, they fell asleep tangled together like the sheets. When he woke, the sun was lower and his stomach louder.

He kissed the top of her head where it rested on his chest. "Get up, woman. I'm wasting away here."

He would've liked to take a shower with Penny before they got dressed. But the bathroom was down the hall and she was worried someone would see them coming or going and spread gossip. He thought it was a little too late for that.

"Reba gave me the snickerdoodles. I'm sure she knows I've been here all morning. What do you think she thinks we've been doing?"

Penny wiggled into her jeans, which was one of the most enticing things Cru had ever witnessed. "You've been trying to talk me into coming back to the ranch. At least, that's my story and I'm sticking to it. But it won't fly if we get caught coming out of the bathroom together all water-slicked from a shower."

He slipped up behind her and pulled her into his arms to nuzzle her neck. "That's too bad. Because I really like the idea of getting all water-slicked with you. What about if I go to the bathroom first and you come later?" When she hesitated, he thought he had her talked into it. But then she shook her head.

"Nope. Miss Gertie might be close to a hundred, but she has the hearing of a hunting dog. And her room is right next to the bathroom."

Cru didn't really believe a woman that old had good hearing, but Penny seemed to believe it. As they were leaving, she pointed to the closed door at the end of the hallway and held a finger to her lips.

He played along and tried to be as quiet as possible as they past. They hadn't even reached the turn off to the lobby when the door swung open and a little shriveled up woman shuffled out holding onto a bright pink walker with a flowered bike basket on the front. In the basket was the butt ugliest cat Cru had ever seen. It was a gray, skinny, hairless thing with huge bulging eyes that looked at him with disgust.

As soon as Penny saw the old woman, she came to attention like a soldier under inspection and stammered out a greeting. "H-Hello, Miss Gertie. How are you today?"

"Dying." It wasn't a joke. The woman looked like she was one step away from death's door. She was nothing but bones, wrinkled skin, and age spots. Although the eyes that turned to him looked intense and alert. "Who are you?"

"This is Cru Cassidy, Miss Gertie," Penny jumped in. "He was helping Chester and Lucas for a while and now he's working on the Gardener Ranch. He just stopped by to try and talk me into coming back."

Gertie glanced at Penny and scowled. "For over

four hours?" She turned to Cru and rolled closer. So close that one walker wheel ran over the toe of his boot. She stared him down. Or more like up since she was so small. He couldn't help fidgeting. If he had on a hat, he would've taken it off. Instead, he bowed subserviently.

"Nice to meet you, ma'am."

She snorted. "You're been up to no good, haven't you, boy?"

He wasn't a good liar. Especially to an old grandma. But Penny must've read his hesitation and adamantly shook her head. He looked back at Gertie and tried to give her an answer without actually lying. "You know how stubborn these Gardeners are. I gave her four hours of lip service and she still won't come back to the ranch." He thought she'd think lip service was talking, but the old gal must've known better because she tipped back her head and laughed.

It was a scary cackle that seemed to come up from the bowels of hell. It cut off as quickly as it had erupted. She pointed a crooked finger at him. "I'll expect you to do right by her. She might've fallen for your slick-talk, but she's a deep down good girl." She turned the crooked digit to Penny. "And you stop giving away the honey before the hive has been bought. Ain't that right, Butler?" She patted the cat on the head before she wheeled her walker around, running over Cru's other foot, and disappeared back into her room. After the door slammed, Penny released her breath.

"That woman and her cat Rhett Butler scare the

crap out of me."

"That makes two of us." Cru took her arm. "Let's get out of here before she comes back."

Since the pharmacy only served breakfast and lunch until two and it was well after three, they had to drive a good thirty miles to a Sonic drive-in. Cru had never cared for Sonic hamburgers, but they did have damn good tater tots and strawberry shakes. Or at least the strawberry shake tasted good when sipped off Penny's lips.

She drew back from the kiss. "Would you stop kissing me so we can eat? I thought you were hungry."

"I am, but not for food as much as . . . honey."

She laughed and shoved a tater tot into his mouth. "Eat." She smiled seductively. "You'll get more honey when we get back to Reba's. Although you'll have to slip into my room through the garden door. We can't chance running into Miss Gertie again."

He leaned over the console and took another strawberry sip from her lips. "Luckily, I'm real good at slipping into places."

On the way back to Simple, he took a shortcut on a back road. It was a bumpy ride, but if it got him into Penny's bed faster, he was willing to deal with a few little bumps.

Or not so little.

About five miles from town, he got on a road that looked like it had been washed out in the last rainstorm. The front tires dipped down into a small gully before he saw it. The jarring jolt had him reaching out to hold Penny in her seat even though she was belted in.

Once they were over the gully, he stopped the truck and turned to her. "You okay?"

"I'm fine, but I don't know if your truck is." She shut the glove box, which had bounced open, then reached down for something on the floor. When she lifted the envelope, his heart felt like it stopped.

He snatched the letter from her hand. "Let me get that." He opened the console and flipped it in, then slammed the lid shut. And when he glanced at her and saw the hurt in her eyes, he knew what she was thinking even before she spoke.

"It's okay, Cru. I know you probably have other girlfriends."

"No, Penny. It's not a letter from a girl. It's a letter to Father Stephen. Sister Bernadette found it after the priest died and thought I would want it." He started driving again and tried to change the subject. "You want to listen to the radio?" He turned on the radio, but she turned it back off.

"Father Stephen died? You didn't tell me that."

"Yeah, well, it's not a big deal." Except it had felt like a big deal when he'd walked into the room and seen the only father he'd ever known laid out in a coffin. He'd been gutted. And Penny knew it.

"Of course it's a big deal." She reached over and placed her hand on his arm. "I know you loved him, Cru. I can tell by the way you talk about him. Did you get a chance to say goodbye? Is that what the letter is? Is it your last goodbye?"

"I didn't get a last goodbye. I was in South Padre

learning how to kite surf when Father Stephen got ill. By the time I found out, he was already gone."

Penny soothingly rubbed his arm. "I'm so sorry, Cru."

He was sorry too. His hands tightened on the steering wheel. "I should've been there."

"You didn't know. If you had known, you would've been there for him."

He looked over at her. "How do you know that? How do you know that I wouldn't have just continued to party on the beach?"

"I know because you're still here. You could've left a long time ago. But you stayed to take care of Chester and Lucas. You stayed to make sure they're okay. I know you would've done the same for Father Stephen." She was only partly right. His concern for Chester and Lucas was one of the reasons he was still there. The woman looking at him with soft, trusting blue eyes was the other. "What's in the letter, Cru? And why are you so protective of it?"

He turned away and looked back at the road. "I'm not protective of it. In fact, I plan to throw it in the trash. I just haven't had a chance."

"I don't believe that. If you brought it with you from Dallas, you've had plenty of chances to throw it away."

He kept his eyes on the road and a tight grip on the steering wheel. "Okay, so maybe I brought it with me. But that doesn't mean anything." His chest tightened, but he ignored the pain and kept driving. He didn't realize he was rubbing his chest until Penny squeezed his arm.

"It's okay to be upset that a man you cared about is gone, Cru. It's okay to want to cherish the last letter you wrote to him."

It was the deep sympathy in her eyes that set him off. Or maybe it was the word "cherish" that did it. "I don't cherish the fuckin' letter. I don't cherish anything from a woman who didn't even care enough to keep her only son. She leaves me in a bus station bathroom and doesn't try to find me for twenty-six years. Then suddenly she tracks me down and leaves her contact information with Father Stephen." He laughed, but even he knew it sounded hollow and forced. "What does she expect? Does she expect me to call her up and say 'Hey, Mom, long time no see?' Well, fuck her and the little horse she rode off on. She didn't give a shit about me and I don't give a shit about her."

His grip tensed even more on the steering wheel as he tried to breathe. But like that day at the Double Diamond Ranch, his lungs refused to draw in air.

"Stop," Penny said.

"Yeah, you're right," he panted. "Who wants to talk about this crap?"

"No, I mean pull over and stop."

She was right. He needed to pull over before he passed out and wrecked the truck. He didn't care about himself, but he cared about Penny. He pulled to the side of the road and expected her to jump out so she could drive. Instead, she crawled right over the console and onto his lap. She looped her arms around his neck and pressing her face to his chest.

"It's okay. It's going to be okay." She squeezed him tightly. It took the dampness seeping through his shirt before he realized she was crying. He wanted to tell her to stop. He wanted to tell her that a stupid letter wasn't worth her tears. That he wasn't worth them.

But Penny thought he was.

Just like Father Stephen and Chester and Lucas, she thought he was worth it. And damned if he could tell her different.

So he just sat there as she held him and her tears soaked through his shirt.

She'd already broken her promise. She'd let him hurt her.

# Chapter Twenty

PENNY SAT AT THE LITTLE glass table in her room at the boardinghouse and watched through the open French doors as a bee pollinated a bright red flower in Reba's garden. As she watched the bee snuggle in to the closed petals, she couldn't help wishing Cru were there to snuggle with her. But she hadn't seen him since her sobbing exhibition the day before. He'd acted like it hadn't bothered him. After she cried herself out, he'd brushed the tears from her cheeks and given her soft kisses. Then he'd brought her here and dropped her off, making the excuse that he needed to go to the ranch for a shower and would come back later. She'd stayed up the entire night waiting for him to walk through the French doors she'd left unlocked.

He never did.

She couldn't blame him. She'd promised him she could handle an adult relationship. And then she had turned into a blubbering idiot over nothing more than a letter.

Tears stung the backs of her eyes at just the thought of the letter. Cru said he cared nothing about his mother—that he didn't want to contact her. But she knew it wasn't true. He wanted to contact her. He was just terrified of getting hurt again. As terrified as he was of hurting her.

Unfortunately, it was too late for that. She had promised him she wouldn't be hurt when he left. But after less than a day of being away from him, she already felt like her heart had been hollowed out. She loved him. Not with the infatuation of a teenager, but with the all-encompassing love of an adult woman who had seen the wounded heart behind the charming playboy smile. She wanted to heal that heart. She wanted to heal it and then she wanted to steal it like he had stolen hers. Unfortunately, he guarded it much too closely for that to ever happen. She knew Cru cared about her. He'd proved it by the way he made love to her. But she also knew that, like her father, he might never be able to express that love.

The bee continued to dance among the wild-flowers. Instead of watching it and feeling sorry for herself, Penny should get dressed and look into finding a job. Sadie had called and said her father was moping around like he'd lost his best friend, but he hadn't tried to contact her and apologize. And she doubted he would. It seemed she was surrounded by mule headed men who couldn't express their true emotions. She needed to accept it and move on.

She started to get up to take a shower when she

noticed two eyes peeking out at her from the thick leaves of the flowers. A second later, a cute little golden-brown rabbit popped its head up.

"Well, good morning," she said.

The rabbit twitched its tufted ears and looked like it was about to answer back when Devlin stumbled into view, causing the rabbit to disappear. Devlin grabbed onto the stalk of a sunflower to keep from falling and snapped the entire flower off. She held it awkwardly in her hand and blushed.

"Good morning, Ms. Gardener. I didn't realize you were staying at this hotel. Although it isn't a hotel as much as a bed and breakfast. Which is what they should call it. Boardinghouse seems a little antiquated and not very appealing from a marketing standpoint."

Cru had explained how he knew Devlin so Penny wasn't jealous anymore, but the woman's bluntness was still a little hard to take. "Reba's family has run this same boardinghouse in Simple for over a century. To change the name would be to take away an important piece of our history."

Devlin nodded as if she'd just been given a crucial piece of information. "Oh well, then that explains it. It looks like I need to do some more research—not just on the surrounding ranches, but on the town." She lifted the cellphone in her hand and looked at Penny. "Are there any books you can recommend that would help me become more knowledgeable?"

Was this woman for real? Penny shook her head. "You are a piece of work."

Devlin looked confused for a second before she tapped away on her phone. "'A piece of work' is slang for a person who is unpleasant, dishonest, hard to deal with, or of low character." She looked at Penny and her cheeks turned pink. "Oh."

Well, dang. Now Penny felt like an unpleasant low character.

"I'm sorry," she said. "I didn't mean that. I'm just upset because my daddy spoke to you about drilling on our property without talking to me first and we got in a big fight."

"Is that why you're here? You fought with your father?"

"That and it was about time I moved out." She waved her in. "Come on in and join me. Reba just brought me a breakfast tray and there's no way I can eat all these scones by myself."

Devlin hesitated for only a moment before she stepped in the open French doors with the sunflower. Penny noticed her cowboy boots and smiled. They weren't a pair she would've chosen, but they were much better than spiked heels. Especially for a woman who was a little unstable on her feet.

"I see you got yourself a pair of boots," she said. "How do you like them?"

"Much more comfortable than heels." Devlin held up the turquoise boot with the red hearts stitched on the sides. "The salesgirl in Abilene talked me into this color, but now I'm wondering if they're a little too flamboyant. What do you think?"

"As long as you like them, that's all that matters."

Devlin lowered her boot and took a chair, setting the sunflower on the table next to the plate of scones. "Shoes and clothing don't really matter to me. I joined an online monthly clothing club with a stylist that picks out all my clothing for me. There was no question on the questionnaire asking if I was a klutz. Which is why my stylist keeps sending me high heels."

"Why don't you send them back so they'll know you don't like them?"

"Because most women my age do love pretty high heels and I was hoping to fit in. In case, you haven't noticed, I'm a little socially awkward."

Her blunt honesty made Penny feel even guiltier for being such a jerk to her. "Well, most women around here don't care about fancy shoes or clothes. They just want you to be yourself." She picked up the plate of lemon poppy seed scones and offered her one.

"No, thank you. Reba brought me some this morning too and I found them a little dry." Devlin cringed. "Obviously, being myself is not a good idea. I always say whatever I think without any thought of hurting people's feelings. I'm sorry. Reba is probably your friend."

"Actually, she's is, although she's closer to my sister. But there's nothing wrong with stating the truth. While Reba's cooking is amazing, her baking has always left something to be desired." She picked up her tea and took a sip. "I have the opposite problem. I'm so worried about hurting people's feelings I rarely speak the truth. And when I finally do, I end up having to leave the only home I've ever known."

Devlin studied her. "If you could do it again, would you tell the truth or would you continue to hide your feelings?"

It was a good question. One Penny knew the answer to. "I'd probably continue to hide my feelings. I miss the ranch. And I'm terrified of never going back to it."

"Is it the actual ranch you miss or what it represents? Home. Security. Family."

Devlin obviously believed in cutting to the chase, and the truthfulness of her words smacked Penny in the face like a hard slap. She wasn't as scared of never going back to the ranch as she was scared of never feeling the security she'd felt when her mother was alive and she, her father, Evie, and Penny were one big happy family. Since Evie had left, she'd desperately tried to recapture that feeling by trying to get her sister to come back and live at the ranch.

But even when Evie had been living there with Clint, they hadn't been a happy family. Not when Evie and her father had constantly been battling. Evie had figured out she needed to make a life of her own and move on, while Penny had tried to cling to the ranch and the past like her only lifeline.

Unfortunately, you can't go back. Even when life doesn't turn out the way you want it to. Mothers are going to die. Fathers are going to be bullheaded control freaks. Sisters are going to move away. And men you fall in love with are going to break your heart. You can either weather life's bumps in the road and fight for your future happiness, or you can hide your head and live in the past.

Penny was tired of living in the past.

She got up from the table. "You're more than welcome to stay and enjoy the garden. But after your wake-up call, I can't sit here feeling sorry for myself. I've got some things I need to do."

Devlin stood and picked up the sunflower. "A wake-up call? I'm afraid I didn't leave you a wake-up call. Perhaps Reba did. But I need to go too and stop by the county surveyor's office. There seems to be some inconsistencies in the map they gave me."

After Devlin's earlier confusion about the property lines, Penny wasn't so sure it had to do with the map as much as Devlin's sense of direction, but she didn't point that out.

Devlin moved to the French doors. "Will you be at dinner tonight? Maybe we could sit together. Last night, Reba sat me next to Miss Gertie. And well, she's kind of . . ."

"Terrifying?" Penny laughed when Devlin hesitantly nodded. "Yeah, she terrifies everyone. And as the oldest resident of Simple, I guess she's earned the right. But that doesn't mean I don't try to hide from her. Save me a seat at supper . . . as far away from her as we can get."

Devlin smiled brightly. "Okay. I will."

Once Devlin was gone, Penny took a quick shower and got dressed before she headed to the

Gardener Ranch. Since it was well after breakfast, she figured she'd have to hunt her father down. But as soon as she hopped out of the truck, he stepped onto the front porch.

"Well, it's about time you came to your senses and got back to work," he said. "All hell broke loose this morning. I had a buyer call me and tell me he's going with someone else for his beef because he found a better deal. The website you wanted me to pay an arm and a leg for isn't working. And a ranch hand quit."

She moved up the steps of the porch. "That does sounds like a bad morning. But in case you don't remember, I quit yesterday."

"That's pure nonsense. You don't quit your family. You're just mad at me for not telling you about the energy company contacting me."

"I *was* mad, but now I'm not mad as much as resigned to the fact that it's time for me to go. I love you, Daddy." She leaned in and kissed his cheek. "You and Mama gave me the best childhood a girl could ask for. So good that I wanted to hang onto it forever. But little girls have to grow up. It just took me longer than most to figure that out."

His eyebrows lowered. "You belong here on the ranch."

"You did convince me of that. You convinced me I wouldn't be happy anyplace else. But that's just not true. It's not true for Evie and it's not true for me. You remember what Mama used to say? She used to say, 'Everyone is responsible for their own happiness.' After she died, I totally forgot her

wise words. I thought you and Evie were responsible for my happiness. I thought if I could just get
you to stop fighting and get along—if I could just
get Evie to move back here and we could live on
this ranch together—we'd be that big happy family
we used to be before Mama died. But even if you
and Evie got along and she and Clint moved back,
it still wouldn't be the same. Because Mama's gone
and Evie grew up. And it's time for me to grow
up too, Daddy. It's time for me to be my own person and not your shadow that follows you around
everywhere."

For the first time in a long time, she saw a glim-
mer of regret in her father's eyes. "If you're gonna
be stubborn about it, I won't let them drill."

"It was never about the drilling, Daddy. It was
about treating me as an equal."

"An equal? Of course you're my equal. You're a
damn good rancher just like your daddy."

She smiled. "Thank you, but that's not going to
change my mind about leaving. It's time. It's time
for me to be own person. But it's not like I'm
moving out of the country. Until I figure out what
I want to do, I'm staying in Simple and I'll be by to
visit every day. And if you need help, all you have
to do is ask."

His face took on the stubborn look she knew
so well. "If you don't come back now, don't come
back at all."

She laughed. "The tough cowboy persona might
keep Evie away, but it won't keep me. I'll be back
whether you want me or not. I'm your daughter

and you won't get rid of me that easily. Besides, Clint is coming this summer and I'll want to spend as much time with him as I can."

His face lit up with surprise. "Clint's still coming?"

"Yes, but he won't be staying long if you can't lighten up a little. You growl too much at him and Evie will take him back to Abilene so fast it will make your head spin."

He stared down at his scuffed cowboy boots for a few minutes before he nodded. "Thank you. I know you're the one who talked her into it."

"Hey, I'm the mediator of the family. It's my job to try to keep everyone happy. I just have to remember to make myself happy too."

He lifted his gaze and stared at her with eyes as blue as hers. "You're just like your mama. She was the peacekeeper. The one who could walk into a room and soften the hardest heart with just a smile."

It was the best compliment he'd ever given her and she'd take it. "Thank you, Daddy. That means a lot." She leaned in to give him a hug.

Usually, she did all the hugging. This time, his arms came around her for a tight squeeze. It only lasted a second, but that was enough. "You'll be back," he said as he drew away. "Ranching is in your blood."

It was. But, at least for now, she wouldn't be ranching here.

She hooked her arm through his. "Come on inside and I'll take a look at that website. Then we'll see if we can't find you another ranch hand. Who quit?"

"Cru Cassidy."

Everything in Penny froze. "Cru left?"

"I don't think he's left yet. He just quit this morning. And if he hadn't quit, I would've fired him. The cocky cowboy had the gall to tell me to stop being a stubborn jackass and apologize to you because I'd never find another ranch manager as good as you are."

If Penny's heart hadn't been hurting so much, she might've laughed at the image of Cru telling off her daddy. But Cru leaving was no laughing matter. She released her father's arm. "I'll be back. There's something I need to tell Cru before he goes."

She found him in the bunkhouse packing a duffel bag that sat on one of the bunks. When he saw her, his hand with the socks in it froze. He looked as sad as she felt. Which should make her feel better, but didn't.

"You came back," he said. "That's good."

She moved closer, her boot heels echoing on the cement floor. "I'm not staying. I just came to pack the rest of my things."

"So you aren't going to work things out with your dad." He threw the socks into his duffel. "Damn, he's such a stubborn ass."

"True, but I've come to realize you can't change people. You can only change yourself."

He looked at her. "You don't need to change. You're perfect the way you are."

"Thank you, but I'm far from perfect. I've spent most of my life trying to make people happy by telling them what they want to hear rather than telling them the truth." She moved closer. "I made you a promise I had no business making. I promised I wouldn't let you hurt me. But in order not to get hurt, you have to keep from getting emotionally involved. And I was emotionally involved with you from the moment you rescued me and tried so hard to keep me from feeling embarrassed about being thrown off a horse. That emotion grew when you came back and I got to know the man behind the teen idol face and teasing smile. And I'm not sorry. I'm not sorry for falling in love with—"

He cut her off, his eyes pained. "Penny, please stop."

"No. I can't keep my emotions bottled up anymore, Cru. I can't pretend not to be hurt because I don't want to hurt you. I'm hurt. I'm brokenhearted that you're leaving. And if that hurts you, then you'll just have to deal with it. But you need to realize that it's your choice this time. This time, you're the one choosing to leave someone who loves you with all her heart."

She didn't wait for him to reply before she turned and walked out.

She was through with waiting around for men to show their love. She was ready to be responsible for her own happiness.

# CHAPTER TWENTY-ONE

CRU WATCHED PENNY WALK OUT the door and the pain in his chest returned. He wanted to grab his bag and try to outrun it like he always did. But, this time, it didn't feel like a giant fist squeezing his heart. This time, it felt like someone had pulled his heart right out of his chest and left a big, gaping wound. And all he could do was sink down on the bed and pray that he died quickly and was put out of his misery.

Instead, God sent two demons from hell to harass him.

"You just had to do it, didn't you, boy?" Chester said. "You just had to charm your way into that little gal's heart and then break it. If you were fifteen, I'd take you out to the woodshed and paddle your ass. Now, I'm going to have to beat the sass out of you with my fists."

Lucas snorted. "You couldn't beat your way out of a paper bag, you old fart. Besides, it already looks like Cru's been beat. What's the matter with you, boy? You're chugging like a steam-engine train after a long haul."

"I think I'm dying." Cru closed his eyes and massaged his chest.

The mattress dipped. "And when did you realize this? Was it before or after Penny walked out that door with tears the size of acorns rolling down her cheeks?"

His eyes flashed open. "She was crying?" He sat up and cracked his head on the top bunk, then fell back and covered his face with his hands. "Of course she was crying. I hurt her. I hurt her badly." He removed his hands and looked at Chester. "Go ahead. Kick my ass. I more than deserve it for breaking her heart. Or better yet, just shoot me and put me out of my misery."

"Don't tempt me," Chester growled.

Lucas got up from the bed. "No one is shooting anyone until Cru explains what happened. Although, now that I see that duffel sitting there, I can probably put two and two together. So you were planning on running off like a sneaky hound dog who just killed all the chickens in the coop?"

That was exactly what he'd plan to do. He'd planned to sneak off without saying goodbye to the Diamond brothers or Penny. And if he'd succeeded, he wouldn't be sitting there with a hole in his chest the size of Texas trying to explain himself to Chester and Lucas. He'd be on his way to sunny California where the women . . . weren't anything like a fiery-haired cowgirl with eyes the color of a summer sky.

"I'm not good at goodbyes," he said as he sat up.

"I figured it was best if I just left."

"That's a coward's way out," Chester said. "Ain't nobody good at goodbyes, but that doesn't mean you just run off without saying them. Folks who care about you have a right to a goodbye. Penny had a right to a goodbye. Even if you don't care about her as much as she cares about you."

"I care about Penny. I'm not leaving because I don't feel the same way she does. I'm leaving because I do. Because she deserves better than an orphaned delinquent deadbeat who still doesn't have his shit together."

The punch took him completely by surprise. He grabbed his jaw and stared at Lucas who was shaking his hand. "What the hell?"

"Yeah," Chester said. "I wanted to hit him."

Lucas didn't acknowledge his brother. His gaze was pinned on Cru. "Don't you ever belittle one of my boys in front of me again. Even if it's you. Now, I realize you haven't yet reached your full potential, but you are not a deadbeat. A deadbeat wouldn't stay with a couple of old men and help them out. He wouldn't sell his fancy car so he could put money in on building them a new house. He wouldn't work his butt off on a ranch that isn't even his because he likes a girl and is too stubborn to accept it. Too stubborn to accept what a good man he is."

Cru released his breath and ran his hands through his hair. "Not good enough for Penny."

"Shouldn't she be the one who's the judge of that?"

"She's in love. She's not thinking straight."

Chester moved closer. "I really do want to punch some sense into you, boy. You should be thanking your lucky stars that she's in love with you and not thinking straight. Instead, you're sitting there looking like a whupped pup moaning about how you're not good enough for her. So get good enough!" He pointed a finger at him. "Because if you let Penny slip through your fingers, it will be the worst day of your life. I should know because I let the love of my life slip through my fingers. Instead of grabbing that woman and making her mine, I was convinced she'd be much better off without a good-for-nothin' rodeo cowboy like me. And look where that thinking got me." He nodded at Lucas. "Stuck with this old coot for the rest of my born days. You want that for yourself, boy? You want to spend the rest of your days regretting not grabbing love with both hands when you had the chance?" He kicked Cru's boot. "If that's what you choose, you are a deadbeat. Come on, Lucas. We shouldn't be wasting our time on a fool."

But Lucas didn't follow his brother. Instead, he waited for Chester to leave before he released a sigh and moved over to the window. "He's right, you know. Love shouldn't be taken for granted. Whenever it's offered, it should be accepted and cherished like the rare gift it is. Chester isn't the only one who lost a love he should've hung on to with both hands." He turned to Cru. "I know you had a tough childhood. I know you put on that big smile and act like everything is okay when inside you're scared to death. It's okay to be scared, Cru. But it's not okay to let that fear keep you from living life. Stop using your head and learn to trust your heart. That might be what's it's trying to tell you." He turned and walked out.

Cru lay back down on the bed and covered his eyes with his arm. He felt like he had been in the worst fight of his life. His chest hurt. His jaw throbbed. And his stomach felt like it was going to revolt at any second. He had been so convinced leaving was the right thing to do. But isn't that what his mother had thought? Hadn't she thought the right thing to do was to leave? And it hadn't been. It had been the worst thing for him. And if what she'd said in the letter was true, it had been the worst thing for her as well. What would've happened if she had made the decision to stay? What would've happened if she'd decided to not give up, but to fight for him? To fight for love?

And maybe that's what she was doing now. Maybe she was trying to fight for love. His love.

He sat up and pulled his cellphone out of his duffel. Before he could change his mind, he quickly dialed the number he'd memorized from all the times he'd stared at the letter. She didn't answer and he thought about hanging up. Then a female voice came through the receiver.

"Hey, y'all. I can't come to the phone right now because I'm either outside in my garden or I can't fine my phone and cussing a blue streak. But as soon as I come in or find the dang phone, I'll call you back."

Cru didn't know what he'd expected, but it wasn't a friendly voice that made him smile. The beep startled him and he realized it was his turn to talk. But all the words seemed to get jumbled in his head and there was a lot of dead air before he finally spoke.

"This is Cru Cassidy." With nothing else to say, he hung up. Before he could even put his phone back in his duffel, it rang. He glanced at the number, surprised she had returned his call so quickly. He tapped the accept button, his stomach a tight ball of nerves.

"So I guess you found your phone," he said.

She laughed a nervous laugh that said she felt as awkward as he did. "I'm always losing things. If it's not my phone, it's my keys. Or even my car in the grocery store parking lot."

"And your son in a bus station." The words just popped out, but he didn't apologize for them.

After a moment's hesitation, she spoke. "Yes, even my son. And before I lost you, I lost myself. And it's taken me a long time to find me." He expected her to go back over all the excuses she'd given Father Stephen in her letter, but she didn't. "I know you hate me. And you have every right to. What I did was inexcusable. And I wish I could turn back the hands of time and do things differently. But I can't. All I can do is say I'm sorry. I'm sorry for not being strong enough to keep you. Whether you believe it or not, I love you. Every single day for the last twenty-six years, I've started my morning out with a prayer that God will watch out for you and surround you with people who love you too. I hope he listened to my prayers."

Cru thought about Father Stephen and the nuns at the St. James's Home for Children. He thought about Chester and Lucas and all the Double Diamond boys. And he thought about Penny.

"Yes," he said. "He listened."

She released her breath in a sigh. "Thank you, Lord." There was a long pause. "I know you can't forgive me, Cru. And I know you don't want me in your life. But do you think I could check in with you every once in a while. I won't bug you a lot. Just every now and again to say 'hi' and see how you're doing."

He hadn't forgiven her, but maybe one day he could. "Sure."

There was another long stretch of silence before she spoke. "So how are you doin'?"

He didn't know her well enough to tell her how he truly felt so he lied. "I'm doin' good. I'm working on a ranch right now."

"In Texas?"

"Is there any better place to be working on a ranch?"

She laughed. "Not as far as I'm concerned. As hard as Texas has been on me, I wouldn't want to live anywhere else. And I've always wanted to live on a ranch or farm where I could grow a huge garden. So tell me about it."

He started telling her about the Gardener Ranch. She was easy to talk to and pretty soon he was telling her other things. He told her about the St.

James's Home for Children, the Double Diamond Ranch, and Chester and Lucas. Finally, he told her about Penny. It was weird, but as he talked, the pain in chest eased—like a large weight had been lifted from it. Maybe it was the weight of hate and anger he'd carried around for so long. Now he just felt sad for a woman who had felt like she had no other choice but to leave her son.

"This Penny sounds like a kind-hearted woman," she said.

"She is. Too kind hearted. She sets herself up to get hurt."

"And are you one of the people who hurt her?"

He sighed. "I didn't want to. She's the last person in the world I'd want to hurt."

"And yet, you did. Believe me, I understand."

And he realized that she *did* understand. She had done the exact same thing. She had hurt the one she loved the most. All because she had convinced herself Cru would be better off without her. And now he was doing the same thing to Penny: letting her go because he didn't think he was the man she deserved. And that was bullshit. If Penny thought he deserved her love, that was all that matter.

"Chester was right," he said. "I am a fool. Instead of sitting here moaning about not being worthy of Penny's love, I should be doing what it takes to become worthy. Listen, I need to go."

It was easy to hear the joy in his mother's voice. "I'll be praying for you . . . son."

The word made his chest feel even lighter. "Thanks, Mom."

Once he hung up, he started to call Penny to tell her how stupid he'd been and how much he loved her and wanted to spend the rest of his life loving her. But before he punched in her number, he stopped. A worthy man wouldn't tell his woman he loved her on the phone. He would prove how much he loved her. Especially when the jackass had let her walk right out the door and done nothing to stop her.

But how could he prove to Penny how much he loved her? How could he prove to her that he was ready to stop his wanderlust ways and settle down?

# CHAPTER TWENTY-TWO

"IF LOOKS COULD KILL, CRU Cassidy would be pushin' up daisies right about now." Emma continued to fill the red plastic Solo cups that sat on the long buffet table with lemonade. "What happened to the pitiful woman who kept me up all night sobbing her heart out and eating all my chocolate chip ice cream?"

Penny pulled her gaze away from Cru's sun-bronzed back and continued to uncover the dishes everyone had brought to Chester and Lucas's house raising. "She's come to realize that Cru Cassidy isn't worth her tears. He's a selfish bastard who can't commit to any woman, and if it wasn't for all the witnesses standing around, I'd pick up one of those hammers and save the rest of the female population some grief."

Emma stopped pouring lemonade and picked up a cup. "If you want, I can put some rat poison in his lemonade. No one would be the wiser."

Boone reached over her shoulder and took the cup from her hand. "It's so like you to poison a

man when he's just trying to quench his thirst."
He downed the lemonade in three gulps, and then
started choking and clutching his throat as he stag-
gered away.

Emma rolled her eyes at Penny. "I can understand why you fell for Cru. The home grown men
from Simple are extremely immature."

"Cru isn't mature. Mature men don't run from
love."

"Honey, I hate to bring this up. But he doesn't
look like he's running."

Penny looked back at Cru, who was helping
Dylan, Billy, Sam, and her father hoist up one
framed wall of Chester and Lucas's new house.
He had stripped off his shirt earlier, and his muscled chest and shoulders glistened with sweat. His
misshapen cowboy hat shadowed his eyes, but she
knew every time he glanced in her direction. She
could feel it like a punch in the heart.

"Why is he still here?" she asked. "He should be
in California right now, soaking up the sun and
having sex with skinny, Botoxed women."

"You're starting to sound a little vindictive and
whiney, honey. You can't fault the man for doing his
charitable duty by convincing Chester and Lucas
to let us throw them a house-raising party." Emma
released a sigh. "Nor can you fault him for having
a body that would make most women swoon from
heatstroke." She glanced over at Penny. "Now don't
go shooting those daggers at me again. I'm just
making an observation. He's your man."

"He's not mine." Penny ripped the plastic wrap

off a bowl of potato salad, then moved down the table to take the tin foil off a plate of fried chicken. "If he were mine, he would've called me in the last week. But he hasn't called me once. Nor has he stopped by to see me at Dixon's Boardinghouse." And she'd left the garden doors unlocked all week. "Asshole."

"You watch your mouth, Penelope Gardener. Or I'll wash it out with Lifebuoy soap like my mama used to do to me." Gertie came rolling up with her walker. She was dressed in a flowered housecoat and a pair of pink furry slippers.

"Sorry, Miss Gertie," Penny said.

"No, you ain't. Just like you ain't sorry for sneaking that boy into your room and having sexual relationships with him."

Penny stood there with her face burning from embarrassment while Emma choked on a laugh. Rhett Butler leaned out of the Gertie's walker and snagged a chicken wing off the plate on the table before disappearing inside his basket. Completely unaware of her cat's larceny, Gertie kept right on talking.

"Back in my day, a man stayed too long in a woman's room, that was cause for her pa to pull out his shotgun." Her gaze snapped over to Emma. "And what are you snickering about, Emma Johansen?" She pointed a gnarled finger. "Don't think I don't know what you and Boone are doing in that hardware store when no one's lookin'. You act like a couple of alley cats fighting for your territory, but you don't have me fooled." This time Emma didn't cough as much as choke. "Now fix me up a plate and put an extra chicken wing on it for Butler."

Neither she nor Penny mentioned that Rhett Butler had already helped himself. "Yes, ma'am," Emma said as she shot Penny a look and hurried to do the old woman's bidding.

"Don't just stand there lookin' stupid, Penelope Gardener," Gertie said. "Get some of that lemonade to those thirsty carpenters."

Penny didn't want to get lemonade to the carpenters. If she got too close to Cru Cassidy, she was afraid she'd clobber him over the head with a two-by-four. She was over crying for the man and now just angry as hell. How dare he stay in Simple when he'd acted like he was going to leave? How dare he parade around with his shirt off and act like he hadn't broken her heart?

Well, if he could act, so could she.

She grabbed a cookie sheet and filled it with cups of lemonade, then carried it around to all the workers. When she got to Dylan, Cru, and her father, she forced a big smile.

"I brought y'all some lemonade." She handed Dylan and her father the last two cups and then looked at the empty cookie sheet as if she hadn't planned it that way. "What a shame."

Cru had the audacity to grin. "That is a shame." He took off his hat and wiped the sweat from his brow with the back of his arm. There was something about his pale underarm with its smattering of dark hair that made Penny feel lightheaded. "I guess I'll have to come get some of your lemonade later." The heated look he sent her said he wasn't talking about lemonade. But no matter how her body reacted to that look, her mind refused to acknowledge the desire sizzling through her.

"Sorry. I'm all out."

Her father stared at her. "What are you talking about, Penelope Anne? There's three entire pitchers sitting right there on the table."

"I'm sure Cru wouldn't want that. He not a simple lemonade kind of guy."

Cru shrugged. "I don't know about that, Miss Penny. I've kinda acquired a taste for . . . simple lemonade."

Her hands tightened on the cookie sheet, and she had to resist the urge to beat him with it. "Like I said before, I'm all out." She turned and walked away.

By the time the sun started to set, Chester and Lucas's house was framed, sided, and roofed. When all the potluck dishes were gone, Reverend Hopkins from the Methodist church and Reverend Peters from the Baptist church gathered everyone around the new house to say a blessing.

Penny moved in between Chester and Lucas, trying not to look at Cru, who stood on the other side of Chester. It was a losing battle. He had sprayed himself off with a hose and his hair was wet and slicked back. He must've pulled his white t-shirt on while he was still wet because the damp cotton clung to his tempting chest and biceps like a second skin.

"Is there something you wanted, Miss Penny?"

he asked, causing her gaze to dart up to his twinkling green eyes.

"Not a thing," she snapped. She took Chester's and Lucas's hands as the prayer started. When she felt their weathered hands tremble, she knew how overwhelmed by the town's generosity they were feeling. Once the final amen was spoken, she squeezed their hands.

"It's okay to let people show you how much you're loved."

Chester cleared his throat. "Well, they sure did that."

Lucas nodded and wiped at his eyes with a bandanna. "They sure did."

"What's everyone standing around for?" Sadie yelled. "There's a brand new wood floor that needs wearing in. Dale, get your band together. We have some celebrating to do."

The band set up on the porch where someone had strung up some Christmas lights. As dust turned to night, Boone started a campfire in the old fire pit and people pulled Coleman lanterns out of trunks and the beds of pickups and hung them inside and out. Soon, you could see couples dancing the two-step in the windowless living room and kitchen.

Penny didn't feel like dancing. She felt like going home and sulking. And because she knew that Emma and Sadie would put up a fuss if she told them she was leaving, she decided to slink away without telling anyone. She was almost to her truck that she'd parked to the left of the campfire when someone grabbed her wrist and stopped her.

She didn't have to look to know who it was. Cru's touch would always send sparks skittering through her.

"Are you leaving?" he asked.

She turned, but kept her gaze away from his mind-altering green eyes. "I think that's my line. Aren't you supposed to be in California?"

"That was the plan. I planned on hopping in my truck and never looking back, like I've done so many times before." His thumb slid back and forth over the pulse point in her wrist that seemed to be beating out of control. "Your heart's beating awfully fast, Penny."

She jerked her arm away and lifted her gaze. "So what stopped you from leaving?"

His eyes reflected the flickering flames of the campfire like it had all those years ago when she'd snuck over to the Double Diamond to see him. "You."

The snort she released didn't come close to expressing her disgust. "Right. Tell that to someone else, Cru Cassidy. If you stayed for me, then you have a strange way of showing. I haven't seen hide nor hair of you in the last week. No visit. No phone call. No nothing. I didn't even know you were still staying at the Gardener Ranch until Sadie told me. And what did you do to her? Not more than two weeks ago, she was warning me against you. And now she thinks you walk on water."

Cru shrugged. "I just helped her organize the house raising . . . and asked her to help me organize a few other things."

"Well, you've done the house raising. Now you can head on out to California and have yourself a great time." She started for her truck, but he stepped in front of her.

"I'm not going to California, Penny. I'm not going anywhere. For years, I traveled around thinking I was just this footloose and fancy-free guy who didn't want to be tied down to anyone or anything. But the truth is I wasn't footloose as much as terrified. Terrified that if I let myself love anyone, they'd leave me. So I always left first. And it was easy to do until I met a woman I couldn't leave. A woman who taught me what it means to love someone. I love you, Penelope Anne Gardener."

She had wanted to hear those words from him forever. But now that he'd said them, she realized they weren't enough. "I know you love me, Cru. That was never the question. The question is how much? And I think you answered that the other day when you let me walk out without saying a word."

He moved as if to pull her into his arms, but she stepped back. "Oh no you don't. Don't you dare touch me and try to sweet talk me back into your bed and then a few days from now decide you want to leave and give me some crap about not being good enough for me. I'm not falling for that again. You're right. You aren't good enough for me. I want a man who doesn't just love me. I want a man who can commit. I know I acted like I could have sex without commitment. But I figured out

I can't."

"Well, you kinda did," he said with a grin.

"Don't be a smartass."

He forced down his smile, but it still quivered at his lips. "Yes, ma'am."

"Now where was I?"

"I believe you were talking about expecting a wedding ring."

"No, I wasn't. I was talking about needing a commitment."

"But isn't marrying someone the best kind of commitment?"

"Well, yes, but I don't think you're ready—"

He cut her off. "I don't think you know what I'm ready for. I also don't think you should have any buts when you're talking about commitment. If two people love each other and want to spend the rest of their lives together, they shouldn't be afraid of committing to that love." He took something out of his pocket. As soon as he got down on one knee, she knew what it was. "Penny Gardener, will you marry me?" He snapped open the box to reveal the most beautiful square-cut diamond engagement ring she'd ever seen.

She stared at the ring in stunned shock. But before she could get a sound out, Chester came hurrying up.

"Hell fire! Are you proposing to her now, boy?"

Cru rolled his eyes and got to his feet. "I was trying to."

"Lucas! Cru's proposing to Penny right now like some country bumpkin without a brain in his head! And by the stunned look on her face, it ain't going well."

Lucas came hurrying over. And he wasn't the only one. Other people had heard Chester's bellowing and soon the band stopped playing and everyone surrounded her and Cru. Including her father.

"What's going on here?" he thundered.

"Cru is asking Penny to marry him," Sadie said. "And you better keep your mouth shut about it, Hank Gardener, or you'll be finding yourself another cook and housekeeper."

"I won't be threatened, Sadie Truly. Nor will I let any daughter of mine marry some drifter."

"Cru isn't a drifter," Lucas said with pride in his voice. "He's a land owner now."

Her father looked as confused as Penny. "What are you talking about? Cru owns land? Where?"

Chester smiled. "Right here. He just bought the Double Diamond Ranch. Or at least a portion of it. The boys wanted to give us money to rebuild our house, but Lucas and I couldn't take their charity without giving them something in return. So we decided to split the ranch seven ways. We get the few acres that the house and barn sit on and our boys get the rest."

"Your boys?" Her father glanced at Cru. "You were one of the boys who came here that summer?" Before Cru could answer, he turned to Lucas and Chester. "Why, you ornery old cusses. After I offered you my hospitality and helped you rebuild your house, you went behind my back and sold the land I wanted to those delinquents who don't know the first thing about ranching."

Penny finally snapped out of her stunned daze over Cru's proposal. "They weren't delinquents, Daddy. They were just boys who needed some love. And Cru knows enough about ranching to help both of us out in a pinch. If he wants to buy some land and start a ranch, that's his business. Just like me deciding whether I want to marry him is mine."

Her father pointed a finger at her. "Fine. But know this, little girl. If you marry a Double Diamond boy, you'll never come back to the Gardener Ranch."

Cru stepped up. "She doesn't need your land, sir. Even if she decides not to marry me, I'm giving her the land I bought from Chester and Lucas as a gift."

She stared at him. "You bought the land for me?"

"I'm willing to do whatever it takes to make you happy. Even leave, if that's what you want."

"Leave?" Luanne Riddell hollered from the crowd. "Please don't tell me you're going to be as stupid as that heroine in the book we read, Penelope Gardener. Hell, if a man offered me my own ranch, I'd marry him in a New York minute."

"You're right, Lulu," Raynelle said. "A man with a ranch is much better than a man with a butcher shop or a truck filled with Ding Dongs."

"Hush up, you two!" Sadie got after them. "Can't you see the man is trying to propose? And they certainly don't need an audience." She waved her hands. "Come on, everybody, let's get back to the dancing and give them some privacy." When Penny's father started to protest, she hooked an arm through his. "She's not your baby anymore, Hank. Come on. I saved you a piece of apple pie."

When everyone had moved away, Cru shook his head. "Damn, I should've taken you to a nice restaurant in Abilene and given you the ring and the deed."

All she could do was repeat herself. "You bought me land."

He smiled at her. "Someone once told me if you had a piece of Texas and a dream, you could do just about anything." His smile faded. "And I'm afraid that's all I have to offer you right now, Penny. Just land and a dream that one day I'll get enough money collected to build you a house and get a few hundred head of cattle."

She stared at him as the truth dawned on her. Cru hadn't just bought her a ring to show he was ready for a commitment. He'd bought her a dream. A dream she'd had ever since a Double Diamond bad boy had ridden into her life.

"Yes," she said.

His eyes widened. "Yes?"

"Are you deaf?" Lucas reappeared. "She said 'yes.'"

Chester moved up next to his brother with a big grin on his face. "Don't just stand there looking stupid, boy. Kiss the girl and seal the deal before she changes her mind."

"Yes, sir," Cru said before he scooped Penny up

in his arms and kissed her. It wasn't a quick kiss. He kissed her like wanted to keep kissing her for the rest of his life.

Penny was just fine with that.

# CHAPTER TWENTY-THREE

"**S**O I'M THINKING WE SHOULD have at least four bedrooms." Cru used the mesquite stick to draw four squares in the dirt around the rectangle he'd drawn for the family room and kitchen.

"And just who's going to be sleeping in those other three rooms?"

He stopped drawing and glanced over at the woman sitting next to him on the blanket under the big oak tree. Her fiery hair spilled around her shoulders like glowing flames and her blue eyes sparkled like sapphires. The happiness on her face was as visible as the afternoon sun blazing in the sky. And he was going to do everything in his power to keep that look on her face.

He set down the stick and scooted closer. "I was thinking kids," he said hesitantly. "But if you don't want children, that's okay. We could use the rooms for when your sister and nephew visit. Or when Chester and Lucas get too old to live by themselves." Which would probably be a long time off. The two old cowboys were doing quite well health wise and emotionally. They loved their new house and were talking about buying a couple more horses they could actually ride. And they loved having Penny and Cru coming by to visit and check on them daily.

Penny smiled and cradled his face in her hand. "You're a good man, Cru Cassidy. And yes, I want children. I want two precious little boys with their father's kind heart and pasture-green eyes."

He turned his head and kissed her palm. "Then we better make it five rooms because I want two girls with their mama's kind heart and sky blue eyes." He grinned. "And I think one should be named Helen Marie for your mama. And one of the boys Hank William after your daddy. Hopefully giving him a son will make him like me a little better."

"He likes you."

"Really? Is that why he told Raul to saddle up that unbroken Appaloosa for me to ride this afternoon?" He glanced over at the wild horse that was straining against the reins Cru had tied securely to a tree branch.

Penny laughed. "All you had to say was you wanted another horse."

"And show weakness to your father? That's like showing weakness to a hungry wolf. You back down an inch and they'll lunge for the throat."

"Daddy's not going to lunge for your throat. He's accepted that you're my choice." When Cru sent her a disbelieving look, she retracted. "Okay, so maybe he hasn't accepted you yet. But he will. And so will Evie."

"Evie? She doesn't want you to marry me either?" This was not good. Getting Hank to like him was hard enough. Now he had to get Evie's approval too? Penny's family meant everything to her. She wouldn't be happy marrying him without their blessings. "What did she say?"

Penny smiled weakly. "Just that we'll get married over her dead body."

"Great."

She squeezed his arm. "You have to understand how hurt she was when Clint's father left and never came back. She doesn't want the same thing to happen to me."

Cru clenched his fists. "If Evie ever tells you who the Double Diamond boy is who left her and Clint high and dry, I'm going to beat his ass."

"You and me both. Which is probably why Evie won't tell me. And for the life of me, I can't figure it out. Was there anyone you remember talking about her?"

"I think all the boys had a little crush on your sister. Except for Logan. He didn't pay attention to her at all. He'd even get up and leave when I started talking about her. But I'm not worried about who Clint's father is as much as I'm worried about getting your family's approval." He took her hand and linked their fingers. "I want to marry you, Penny, but I don't want to cause problems between you and your family."

Penny brought their linked hands to her chest

and pressed the back of his against her heart. Her gaze was steady and true. "I do love my family, but I spent most of my life trying to make them happy. Now it's my turn and I won't let them stand in the way of my happiness. I want you, Cru. I want to marry you and have pretty babies with you and build a life with you. And the sooner that life starts the better."

"Are you saying you'll marry me today?"

She laughed. "Not today. I might be anxious to become Mrs. Cassidy, but I'm still a girl who wants a beautiful wedding. I'm thinking late summer or early fall under my mama's rose arbor."

Joy burst inside him like an overfilled balloon and he slid his hand through her glorious hair and pulled her in for a leisurely kiss. And then another. And then another. He started to lower her to the blanket, but she stopped him.

"They'll be plenty of time for kisses later. Right now, I want to see the rest of our house."

He gave her one more kiss before he picked up the stick and went back to his drawing. "I'm thinking all the kid's rooms should be on this side of the house and our room will be on this side. I think it should have huge windows on one wall and, on the other, glass doors that lead out to a garden just like the French doors at Dixon's Boardinghouse."

She rested her chin on his shoulder. "Are you going to slip in those doors like you've been slipping into mine every night?"

"I'm going to be slipping into Miss Reba's garden room every night as long as you're there. But

I hope I won't have to sneak into my own house."

"Not unless you do something to make me kick you out."

His eyes widened as he turned to her. "Now, honey, what would make you think that? I plan to be the most devoted husband in the entire state of Texas."

Her eyebrow cocked. "Are you saying I tamed the bad boy?"

"That's exactly what I'm saying."

She snorted. "Bullshit. I think that bad boy is still lurking inside you just waiting to do some naughty things."

"Wishful thinking, Penelope Anne Gardener?"

"You better believe it."

He bit back a grin. "So let me get this straight. I not only have to spend the rest of my life being the straight man for your horrible knock-knock jokes, I also have to be your sex slave?"

She looked thoroughly offended. "My horrible knock-knock jokes? My jokes aren't horrible and I can prove it. Knock-knock."

A smile broke out on his face. A smile that came from the knowledge he would be spending the rest of his life with this woman. "Who's there?"

"Ima."

"Ima who?"

"Ima gonna love you forever, Cru Cassidy."

Cru tipped back his head and laughed before he lowered her down to the blanket and proved beneath the big ol' Texas sky that he intended to do the same thing.

Coming soon Katie Lane's next
Bad Boy Ranch novel,

# Taming a Texas Rebel!

**"I** THOUGHT BIG CITY GIRLS HOT waxed
from their eyebrows to their toes . . . including their womanly petals."

Evie Gardener struggled to hold back her laughter at Raynelle Coffman's inappropriate comment.
Like most folks in Simple, Texas, Raynelle didn't
believe in mincing words. She said what she
thought when she thought it, even if she was
standing at her cash register at the Simple Market.

Ignoring the line of people who had moved
closer to hear her reply, Evie continued to unload
her cart. "Abilene isn't really that big, Raynelle.
It's only a little over a hundred thousand people."
Which *was* big when compared to the little over
seven hundred people who lived in Simple. Seven
hundred who would no doubt hear all about this
conversation by suppertime.

"So you're saying you don't hot wax down
there?" Raynelle slid the razor that had brought up
the topic over the scanner. Evie wanted to ignore
the question, but she knew if she did, the people
standing in line would take that as confirmation

and the gossip would be even worse. It was the one thing she didn't miss about living in a small town.

Probably because she'd been the brunt of gossip most her life.

In Abilene, she was just a single mom who worked as a loan officer at a bank. Here in Simple, she was Evie Gardener who'd had a string of bad luck. *Bless her heart.* She fell off a horse and broke her arm when she was five, dropped her baton five times in the twirling contest when she was ten, lost her mother from heart disease when she was thirteen, and got knocked up by some foreigner from Spain when she was fifteen. Now she lived in a big city and was hot waxing her womanly petals. *Lord have mercy.*

Evie finished unloading her cart and decided to answer truthfully. "Are you kidding, Ray? With a full-time job and a teenage son, I don't have time to hot wax anything."

Raynelle laughed. "I hear you, sister. Raising boys is one tough job—a never-ending job if Clint turns out anything like my Brandon. Of course, that's my own fault. I should've kicked that lazy boy out when he turned twenty-one. Or at least made him do his own laundry and cooking. I guess I'm just a soft-touch where my baby is concerned."

Evie understood completely. Clint was her baby too—the precious boy who could brighten her day with just one smile. Of course, lately, he hadn't been doing much brightening. Her joyful little boy who had loved his mama to the moon and back had turned into an angsty, belligerent teenager who rarely shared a smile or talked with her—probably because she couldn't help turning every conversation into a lecture.

But it was hard not to lecture a kid who refused to keep his room clean or do his homework or stay away from troublemakers. Since entering high school, his grades had plummeted, he'd been arrested for drinking beer in the neighborhood park, and just recently, he'd been given school detention for smoking on campus. He should be on restriction until the cows came home. Instead, she had let him talk her into spending the summer on the Gardener Ranch with her daddy.

She had to be the worst pushover ever. Closely followed by Raynelle.

"Now my son has brought home his girlfriend to live with us. And that lazy girl don't do laundry or cook either." Raynelle held up a bag of Nacho Cheese Doritos. "What are all these snacks for, honey? You plannin' on having an engagement party for your little sister. Everyone in town is excited about Penny marrying that cute Cru Cassidy."

Every muscle in Evie's body tightened. Penny would marry Cru over her dead body. Her sister wasn't ready for marriage. She was too young and naïve. Having spent most of her life under the thumb of their domineering father, she had rarely left the ranch or dated. She was sweet and innocent and believed in the goodness of people. Evie had once believed in the goodness of people too, but she knew better now. And she wasn't about to let her little sister marry a wild Double Diamond boy and end up getting her heart broken.

"There will be no engagement party," she said adamantly. "These snacks are for Clint while he's staying at the Gardener Ranch. The boy can eat his weight in Doritos."

Raynelle seemed a little surprised by the no engagement comment, but she recovered quickly and scanned the chips. "I heard Clint was helpin' your daddy this summer. It's nice he'll get to spend some time with his grandfather."

Evie didn't think spending time with her father was nice, but obviously Clint did. As soon as she pulled up to the ranch, he'd hopped out and greeted his grandfather with a big hug. And daddy had looked just as happy to see him. He'd thumped him on the back and told him all about the Appaloosa horse he had gotten for him. Evie, on the other hand, had only gotten a lecture about not calling to say they'd be late. Of course, she hadn't expected anything different. She and her father were like kerosene and a lit match. Anytime they were together, things usually exploded.

Which is why she'd moved away. But she couldn't deny her son a relationship with his grandfather. Or time spent on the Gardener Ranch. Some of her happiest memories were of living at the ranch. Of course, that was when her mother had been alive to soften her father's stubborn nature.

"You plannin' on staying at the ranch with Clint?" Raynelle asked.

"No, I'm going to stay a few days in town with

my sister before I head home."

Raynelle shook her head sadly. "I was sure sorry to hear about your daddy and Penny having that big fight and her moving out. Both of you girls should be staying at your home instead of Dixon's Boardinghouse." Everyone in line nodded his or her head in agreement.

Rather than air the family dirty laundry, Evie tried to lighten the conversation. "But then I wouldn't get to see you, Raynelle."

Raynelle got a big smile on her face. "Well, there is that."

After Evie paid for her groceries, she carried the bags out to her Camry. She'd bought the Camry used ten years ago and it had reached its expiration date. The air conditioner made a strange squealing sound if you ran it too high, two of the windows wouldn't roll down, and the fuel gauge was broken so she had to guess on when she needed to get gas. She just hated to spend money on a new car when there were so many other things to spend it on.

She put her groceries in the trunk. Since she hadn't bought anything perishable, she didn't have to worry about driving them out to the Gardener Ranch today. She would take them to Clint tomorrow and check to make sure her son still wanted to stay. A day with her grumpy father might be all he needed to change his mind. But right now, she wasn't worried about Clint changing his mind as much as her sister changing hers.

Dixon's Boardinghouse was located on the edge of town. The big plantation-style mansion sat back from the main highway and was surrounded by green lawn and shady oak trees. The house was three stories tall, including the attic rooms, and had been built in the 1800's by a wealthy cattleman for his new bride. The woman had loved the house, but hated the dismal Texas town it was in and had taken the first train back to Chicago she could get.

Not wanting to ruin his wedding plans, Dale Dixon had asked his Cherokee housekeeper to take her place. The marriage had turned out to be an affair of the heart and the couple had had seven children together. Unfortunately, six of those kids had greedily used up all the money and run the ranch into the ground. When the parents passed, all that was left was the house that they willed to the seventh child. With no way to pay for its upkeep, she'd turned it into a boardinghouse. It had been a boardinghouse ever since—except for a short time during the oil boom of the early 1900's when it had been turned into a house of ill repute. Something that Reba's great-aunt, Miss Gertie, refused to talk about.

The tourists who stayed at the hotel loved the history of the boardinghouse as much as they loved sitting on the wide wraparound porch with tall glasses of mint juleps. As Evie climbed the steps, she smiled at the older couple sitting in the white rocking chairs.

"It looks like y'all are having a good afternoon. Nothing like sitting in the shade on a hot Texas day with one of Reba's special mint juleps." She glanced over at the man sitting on the other side of the porch. His cowboy boots were propped on the railing and his black cowboy hat rested at an angle over his face. But it was easy to tell by his fisted hands that he was awake and no doubt ticked she'd disrupted his sleep.

"Pardon me," she said. "My mama always said I could call hogs to supper all the way from Oklahoma with my loud voice." The polite thing would've been for the cowboy to at least acknowledge her apology with a nod. Instead, his hands fisted even tighter. Obviously, he wasn't from around there. She turned away from him and smiled at the couple. "Y'all enjoy your stay in Simple." She opened the screen door and then purposely let it slam shut behind her, hoping it really ticked off the rude cowboy.

Once inside the boardinghouse, she forgot about the man and looked around for Reba. She should've known she'd find her in the kitchen. Reba loved to cook. Which was a good thing since she had to do plenty of it.

"Good Lord, there must be enough chicken pot-pies to feed the entire state of Texas," she said as she entered the kitchen.

Reba whirled from the stove and a bright smile lit her face. "Evie!" She hurried over and pulled her in for a tight hug. Reba had always been the best hugger, her body as soft as her heart.

"Well, aren't you a sight for sore eyes." Reba pulled back and her brow wrinkled with concern. "Okay, what's wrong? I know that troubled look. Is it Clint?"

"It's not Clint this time. This time, I'm more worried about Penny. I guess you heard about her hooking up with Cru Cassidy."

"I sure did. She's been staying here in the garden room."

"With or without Cru?"

"You know my Aunt Gertie wouldn't let any unmarried couples stay here on her watch." Reba paused. "But that doesn't mean that a slick cowboy couldn't slip through the garden doors if he had a hankerin'."

Evie gritted her teeth. "And I'm sure Cru has done plenty of slippin'. Are they here now?" If they were, Cru Cassidy was about to get a piece of her mind. And Penny too for being so gullible. Unfortunately, Reba shook her head.

"They left together early this morning. I guess he found a used house trailer that he wants to buy until they can build a house."

"My sister is not going to move into a house trailer!"

Reba tipped her head. "Lots of good folks live in house trailers, Evie."

"I have nothing against trailers. What I meant is that Penny's not living anywhere with Cru Cassidy."

Reba's studied her for a moment before she glanced back at the simmering gravy on the stove. "Let me get this chicken filling into the rest of the pie shells and then we can get out of this hot kitchen and have us a good talk."

Evie grabbed an apron and helped her by adding

the crust to the top of each pie and crimping the edges. In just a short time, they had the potpies in the commercial-sized oven and were sitting in a canopied swing in Reba's beautiful back garden with big glasses of sweet tea.

"Now do you want to explain why you're so unhappy about Penny falling in love?" Reba asked.

"I want Penny to find someone to love. But true love doesn't happen when you only know a person for a few months. That's called lust. And you can't build a good relationship on lust."

"According to what Penny says, they've known each other since they were thirteen and fifteen. Cru was one of the troubled boys who stayed at the Double Diamond Ranch that one summer."

"I know exactly who Cru Cassidy is. And trouble is exactly the word for all the boys Chester and Lucas took in."

"Which is why I'm upset as heck my mother sent me to fat camp and I missed out on all those delicious-sounding delinquent boys."

"Believe me, you didn't miss anything."

Reba took the lemon slice off the rim of her glass and squeezed it into her tea. "I don't know about that if Cru is any example of the boys who spent the summer there. Besides being faint-worthy in the looks department, he's charming, funny, and a true gentlemen. He saw me starting up the lawn mower the other day and insisted on mowing the entire acre. He looks at Penny like she not only hung the moon but also all the stars. He even won over Aunt Gertie and you know how tough she is to win over."

Evie set her glass on the table next to her. "That's exactly why the Double Diamond boys are so dangerous. They come off as perfectly harmless. Like they're these misunderstood boys who didn't have a fair shake in life. But every single one of those boys deserved to be at a boy's ranch for the summer. Everyone is a wolf in sheep's clothing just waiting to pounce. And I'm not going to let my little sister become a wolf's supper."

Reba smiled. "I wouldn't mind being a wolf's supper. I've always liked my men a little hairy and hungry." She stood. "Speaking of supper, I need to check the potpies and get the salad made."

"I'll help you." Evie started to get up, but Reba waved her off.

"It won't take me any time. You sit right here and enjoy the garden."

It was a beautiful garden—if not a little chaotic. There were flowers and plants of every variety growing with no rhyme or reason. Amid the profusion of color and greenery were gray stone benches, bubbling fountains, statues of garden fairies . . . and a little golden rabbit that looked almost life like. When it twitched its little black nose, Evie realized that it was alive. The rabbit stared at her with its big brown eyes for just a second before it disappeared behind a rose bush.

The big pink roses reminded Evie of her mother's rose garden. Helen Marie Gardener had married into the right name. Her green thumb had been legendary and won her more than a few blue ribbons at the county fair. No flower could die when showered with her mother's love and attention. She'd showered the same love and attention on her two daughters and they had grown and thrived— until their beloved gardening mother had died.

Then it was like the sun had left the garden and the water had all dried up. Like her mother's roses, Evie had wanted to shrivel up and die too. But she couldn't. Not when she had a little sister to care for. So she'd pushed down her grief and become Penny's surrogate mother.

And she wasn't done with her job yet.

She pulled her cellphone out of her purse and glanced at the time. It was close to five o'clock. Surely Penny would be back by now. Evie got up and headed along the path that led to the garden room. She weaved her way through the overgrown flowers, pushing lilac bushes and drooping sunflowers out of the way as she went. Stepping around a rosemary bush that had to be five feet wide, she stopped in her tracks.

A man lay in the hammock strung between two flowering mimosa trees. The same man from the front porch. His booted feet were crossed at the ankles, his hands rested on his stomach, and his black cowboy hat covered his face. After she slammed the screen door, he must've decided the garden would be a quieter place for a nap.

She didn't usually pay much attention to men's bodies. She was too busy working and raising a son to let a few well-placed muscles turn her head. But this man didn't just have a few well-placed muscles. Every muscle seemed to be exactly where it should be.

Broad shoulders and knotted biceps filled out the shoulders and sleeves of his black t-shirt like it had been painted on. His hands rested on a flat stomach that made Evie wish she'd gotten the salad instead of the chicken nuggets when she and Clint had stopped for lunch and his long, lean legs made her wish she'd brought her iced tea with her. Her mouth felt suddenly dry. It got even drier when her gaze settled on the bulge beneath the worn fly of his jeans.

Yes, the man definitely had nice muscles.

The sound of a throat being cleared had her eyes flashing up. With a cringe of embarrassment, she realized that, even though his hat was tipped low over his face, she could still see his eyes beneath the brim's shadow. And if she could see his eyes, he could see her. As she struggled to come up with some plausible excuse for ogling him, he removed the cowboy hat.

The sight of his face had her exhaling in a startled whoosh. The dark brown eyes were as piercing and unrelenting as they'd been fifteen years earlier. The cheekbones as high and chiseled. The lips as stern and unsmiling. When he spoke, his sexy Texas drawl cut right through her.

"Checkin' out my sheep's clothin', Evelyn . . . or the wolf beneath?"

# Be sure to check out Katie Lane's other books!

# About the Author

KATIE LANE IS A USA Today Bestselling author of the *Deep in the Heart of Texas*, *Hunk for the Holidays*, *Overnight Billionaires*, *Tender Heart Texas*, *The Brides of Bliss Texas*, and *Bad Boy Ranch* series. She lives in Albuquerque, New Mexico, with her cute cairn terrier Roo and her even cuter husband Jimmy.

For more on her writing life or just to chat, check out Katie here:
Facebook *www.facebook.com/katielaneauthor*
Instagram *www.instagram.com/katielanebooks*

And for information on upcoming releases and great giveaways, be sure to sign up for her mailing list at *www.katielanebooks.com*!